# THE WHISPERING PAGES

## WHERE STORIES REMEMBER WHAT YOU FORGET

SHIVI SHARMA

To my mom,

for your endless love and faith in me.

And to my friend, Shubh,

for standing by me when the pages got heavy

# Contents

# Acknowledgements

To everyone who turned these pages and chose to walk beside Layla through her quiet, haunting story—thank you.

Writing The Whispering Pages was like chasing shadows and stitching them into light, and I couldn't have done it without the love, patience, and belief of those around me.

To my mom—thank you for grounding me when my imagination flew too far.

To my friends—thank you for listening and encouraging me. I am grateful to you guys.

To every reader who saw a part of themselves in Layla, Ana, or Ryan—this story is yours as much as it is mine.

And to the stories still waiting to be told—

I hear your whispers.

With all my heart,

Shivi Sharma.

# I

# The Quiet Girl

Layla didn't believe in signs — until the world started to write her story.

It was supposed to be an ordinary Wednesday.

Layla walked through the halls of Riverstone High, her footsteps muffled against the worn tiles, her mind already lost in the world of her book. Her dark hair was pulled back into a simple ponytail, her eyes scanning the pages, ignoring the chatter around her. It was easy to get lost in her books. They were her escape from everything — the noise, the questions, the expectations.

"Layla!"

Ana's voice cut through the fog of her thoughts, pulling her back into the present.

She blinked and looked up, meeting Ana Lopez's mischievous grin. Ana was the storm to her calm — a whirlwind of energy that never seemed to stop moving. Where Layla was quiet, Ana was loud; where Layla kept her distance, Ana broke through it without hesitation.

"You look like you're about to disappear into that book," Ana teased, reaching over and tapping the side of Layla's head lightly.

"I'm just trying to survive another day," Layla muttered, closing the book and tucking it into her bag. She wasn't sure if she was talking about school or life in general.

Ana raised an eyebrow, her lips curving into a playful smirk. "You really need to get out of your head, Layla. You're starting to turn into a ghost. How do you even survive lunch like this?"

Layla rolled her eyes. "I survive because I don't have a choice."

"Uh-huh. Sure, sure. Listen," Ana began, her voice suddenly quieter. "If you ever want to actually live, you need to stop hiding behind books. Or me. You're too quiet. It's like no one even knows you're here."

Layla gave her a small, wistful smile. "Maybe that's the way I like it."

Ana shook her head, clearly not agreeing, but not pushing further. The two of them settled down at their usual spot at the corner table of the school's cafeteria , Ana immediately diving into her phone, while Layla pulled out her lunch and opened her book. Silence settled over them, but it wasn't uncomfortable. For Layla, it was normal. This was her life — quiet, steady, with Ana there, breaking up the silence every so often with her loud laugh or random questions.

"So, anything exciting going on in your world?" Ana asked after a few minutes, not looking up from her phone.

Layla chewed her sandwich thoughtfully, not in a hurry to answer. "Nope. Same old stuff. School, home, books. That's about it."

"Isn't that just boring?" Ana asked, glancing up at her with a raised eyebrow. "I mean, you're a mystery. You've been living here for, what, a year now? Don't you want to do something... interesting?"

Layla looked around at the other students, laughing and talking, carefree in a way she could never quite manage. "I don't need to be excited. I have books for that."

Ana tilted her head, her expression softening. "You know, I'm the only one who knows you, right? If I didn't, I'd think you were some kind of... well, not real person. You're here, but not really here."

Layla shifted uncomfortably, brushing a loose strand of hair behind her ear. "I'm here enough."

"Not enough for the rest of the world to notice, apparently," Ana retorted, before her gaze softened again. "But hey, I like you just the way you are."

Before Layla could respond, the bell rang, signaling the end of lunch. The two of them gathered their things in silence and headed toward their next classes.

---

That evening, at home, the quiet was different.

Layla dropped her bag by the door and walked into the kitchen, where her mother, Riya, was chopping vegetables for dinner.

"Hey, Mom," Layla said softly, slipping onto one of the stools at the counter.

Riya looked up, her tired eyes softening as she smiled. "Hey, sweetie. How was school today?"

"Same as usual," Layla replied, giving her a half-hearted smile. "Nothing new."

Riya nodded, but there was a quiet tension in the air — the unspoken strain of the life they were building in the United States. "Your father will be late tonight. He's finishing up some reports. Ayaan's in his room, watching something on TV."

"Okay," Layla said, her voice distant as she fiddled with the edge of her sleeve. Her mom always seemed to be rushing between tasks, and Layla had learned to let her be. There was always something she had to do — work, errands, things she couldn't explain.

"I miss India sometimes," Riya said suddenly, her voice lower, almost wistful.

Layla blinked, surprised. "I miss it too."

There was a long silence between them as Riya continued chopping the vegetables. Layla's thoughts wandered back to the familiar chaos of Mumbai — the crowded streets, the noisy markets, the endless traffic. She missed it too. But what was there to say? They had moved here for a better future, a new start. Wasn't that enough?

"Don't let the silence swallow you whole," Riya said quietly, more to herself than to Layla.

---

Later that night, as the house settled into darkness, Layla sat at her window. The streets of Maplewood stretched out before her — empty, quiet. The only sound was the rustling of leaves as a gentle breeze passed through.

She didn't know why she felt so uneasy. It wasn't like there was any reason for it. Everything was just as it always was. But still, something about tonight felt different. Like something was about to change.

From downstairs, she could hear Ayaan calling for her. "Layla! I need help with my homework!"

She sighed, pushing herself off the windowsill, and walked down the hall to her brother's room. Ayaan was sprawled on the floor, his homework papers scattered around him.

"Need some help, little man?" she asked, sitting beside him.

Ayaan looked up, his dark eyes wide. "Yeah, I don't get this math stuff. It's too hard. I think I'm gonna fail!"

Layla smiled softly, reaching over to help him. "You're not going to fail. You just need to focus."

"You always know what to do," Ayaan said with a grin. "You're like, the smartest person I know."

"I just read a lot of books," Layla replied, laughing softly. "Books are like... instructions for life."

Ayaan rolled his eyes. "You and your books. Maybe you should write your own one day."

"Maybe I will," Layla said, her voice soft, but something flickered in her chest — a strange pull, like the very idea of writing a story was already forming inside her.

---

Layla went to her bedroom and as always started reading her current read- "A good girl's guide to murder" by holly jackson.

Her parents were asleep, and Ayaan had tucked himself into bed, but Layla's mind refused to rest. The world felt different tonight as if a storm was about to come. She closed her book, setting it down beside her. She leaned her head against the cool glass of the window, letting the breeze wash over her face. Outside, the streets of Maplewood were silent, save for the distant hum of the town's single streetlight flickering in the night.

Layla turned off the light and went to sleep knowing she'll have to wake up tomorrow morning early for school.

# II

# Between Pages And People

Maplewood's mornings were always quiet, but that Thursday seemed especially still. The town didn't rush, even when Riverstone High hummed in the background. In the mornings, Layla enjoyed the peace—before the day's noise and energy took hold. Every morning, she had the same routine: wake up early, avoid the chaos, and slip into the world of her own thoughts.

As she made her way to school, the streets of Maplewood felt familiar, a place where the houses seemed to watch over her, their brick walls knowing her name. Layla often thought of how small and close-knit her town was, how everyone knew everyone. She could hardly imagine what it was like to live in a city where anonymity was a thing. Maplewood was different. It was intimate, like a family, but that closeness also made her feel exposed.

By the time she reached Riverstone High, she was already in a zone of calm detachment. She had never been one for crowds or attention. In the bustling hallways of the school, Layla could almost blend into the walls if she tried hard enough. It was where she was safest.

In the first period ; Literature, Layla sat beside Ana Lopez, her best friend, whose infectious energy always seemed to bubble up at the most unexpected times. Ana's pencil darted across the page, filling her notebook with sketches and quotes. Layla envied how free Ana was with her thoughts, always willing to express whatever was on her mind. They had been friends for years, but Ana was still the loud, outgoing one while Layla remained the quiet observer.

"Layla," Mr. Bennet said, glancing over his glasses, "you've read Wuthering Heights, haven't you?"

Layla nodded. "Twice."

Ana, sitting beside her, whispered with a smirk, "Show-off."

Layla shrugged, a faint smile tugging at her lips. Ana always had this way of making her feel like part of the world, even when she didn't want to be.

"And how would you describe Heathcliff in one word?" Mr. Bennet asked.

"Unforgiven," Layla said after a beat, her voice soft but certain.

Ana raised an eyebrow. "That's a new one. I thought you'd say 'brooding' or 'tormented'."

Layla smiled again, a bit more genuinely this time. "I like to think of him as someone who couldn't let go of his pain."

Mr. Bennet nodded, impressed. "Perfect." He turned back to the board. "And that, class, is what makes Wuthering Heights such a compelling story. Heathcliff's inability to forgive and move on creates the tension that drives the novel."

After class, Ana leaned over. "You always have these deep answers. Are you sure you're not a secret poet?"

Layla felt a brief flicker of embarrassment but brushed it off. "Not secret. Just quiet."

"I don't know how you do it," Ana continued. "I would go crazy if I had to be so... I don't know... still all the time."

"I'm not still," Layla said softly, glancing out the window. "I'm just... in my head a lot."

Their day passed in fragments. A joke about the cafeteria food, complaints about Chemistry, and a crumpled paper airplane that Ana had thrown across the lunchroom. Layla caught it mid-air, unfurled the wing, and read: Ana is bored out of her mind. She chuckled and tossed it back.

By the time the final bell rang, Layla could feel the familiar weight of the day settling on her shoulders. Ana had to rush off to debate practice, leaving Layla to her thoughts as she headed down Main Street. The wind had picked up, carrying the scent of rain, and Layla's heart quickened in a way she couldn't explain. She liked the weather, even when it made things feel more uncertain.

As she walked to The Lantern, her sanctuary in the small town, Layla's footsteps slowed, letting the rhythm of the street settle in her bones. The Lantern had always been a safe place for her—a place that didn't demand anything of her, a place where the silence felt like it belonged to her.

The library stood at the end of Main Street, an old building with ivy creeping up its stone walls. The bell above the door chimed softly as she entered, and the warm, earthy smell of books immediately enveloped her. The Lantern was quiet, as always, but there was something about it that felt different today. Something in the air, almost imperceptible.

Mr. Williams, the librarian, greeted her from behind the counter. "Right on time, Miss Singh," he said, a smile playing at the corner of his lips.

Layla smiled back. "I like my habits," she said softly, slipping into her usual routine.

Mr. Williams adjusted his round glasses, peering at her over the top. "Nothing wrong with that," he replied, his voice lower. "I've got a stack of returns for you to browse. Left them near the fireplace alcove."

She nodded and wandered toward the back of the library, where the shelves stretched high above her. The quiet was comforting—drowned out only by the soft ticking of a clock in the far corner and the occasional murmur from Mr. Williams.

Layla found her favorite spot near the fireplace, sinking into the worn red armchair. She pulled out her notebook and began to scribble notes, her mind wandering over the pages of books she'd read. The rain started outside, gentle at first, then harder as the wind howled against the windows.

Her eyes drifted to the small children's section where a mother was reading to her daughter. The picture was peaceful—just another normal afternoon in The Lantern. But something about it felt off, like an unnoticed detail that only she could see.

She turned back to her notes and tried to shake off the feeling.

As time passed, Layla lost herself in the comforting world of books, feeling the warm tea that Mr. Williams had brought her grow cold in her hands. The sounds of the rain outside were soothing, but her thoughts kept slipping back to that odd feeling—the one she couldn't place.

# III

# The Book That Wasn't There

The Lantern always smelled of dust, polished wood, and something older—like forgotten things that wanted to be remembered. The sun slanted through the tall windows, scattering soft gold across the floor. Layla walked slowly between the rows of shelves, her fingers grazing the book spines like they might whisper secrets to her if she touched them just right.

Mr. Williams was humming to himself at the front desk, sorting a stack of returns with his usual slow, methodical rhythm. The library was nearly empty, just the way Layla liked it.

She wasn't looking for anything specific, only wandering. Thinking. Wondering why she hadn't been able to shake the chill from that morning. Or the odd dream from last night—the one where she was inside a book, running down pages that closed behind her.

She turned down an aisle she didn't remember noticing before. It was dimmer, the books older, their spines cracked and faded. At the end of the shelf, something caught her eye—a black book with no title. No author. Nothing. Just worn leather and an odd shimmer when the light hit it.

Drawn to it, she pulled it out carefully. It felt warm in her hands.

The first page was blank. The second, too. Then, finally, the third: Chapter One.

No title. Just text. But the first paragraph—

Layla blinked.

It described a girl walking through a library, finding a book with no name.

She slammed it shut.

"Whoa—didn't mean to scare you."

She turned sharply. A boy stood a few feet away, hands in the pockets of his jacket, his posture relaxed but alert.

"Sorry," he said again, his voice calm. "Didn't mean to sneak up. You looked... kind of frozen."

She recognized him instantly. Ryan Cole. Senior. Basketball team. Mysteriously quiet, except when he wasn't. There were always rumors around him—about how he only talked when it mattered, how he wrote things down more than he spoke, how he once walked off the court mid-game because he "saw something wrong."

Layla wasn't sure what she believed. But he was definitely real, standing there in the back of the library.

"It's fine," she said, hugging the book to her chest. "Just startled me."

He nodded toward it. "Weird one?"

"No title."

"Those are the best ones," he said, stepping closer, his eyes flicking to the dusty shelves. "The kind you don't expect to find, but they find you."

Layla tilted her head. "You a reader?"

Ryan shrugged. "Sometimes. Mostly thoughts. I write them down. Makes it quieter up here." He tapped the side of his head. "Helps after games."

She noticed a notebook tucked under his arm.

"You come here often?"

"Used to," he said. "Then life got busy. But this place..." He glanced around. "It's got a feeling, doesn't it?"

Layla nodded. "Like it's watching you."

"That's not creepy at all," he said with a slight grin. "Mind if I sit?"

She hesitated, then nodded. He sat down at the small table nearby, flipping open his notebook. Inside were scribbles—quotes, sketches, half-drawn basketball plays, and tiny observations in the margins.

Layla opened the book again, tentatively.

Ryan didn't say anything, just let the silence stretch comfortably. It surprised her.

"Do you believe in coincidences?" she asked suddenly.

"Sometimes," he said without looking up. "But sometimes I think we just don't have the language for the patterns yet."

That made her pause.

"The book," she said slowly, "described exactly what I did a few minutes ago."

He looked at her, expression unreadable. "You sure it wasn't déjà vu?"

"No. I mean—maybe. But this felt... like it was written for me."

Ryan didn't laugh. He didn't joke. He just nodded, thoughtful. "Some stories choose their readers."

Mr. Williams called from the front. "We're closing in five, Layla!"

Layla stood, still clutching the book. "I should go."

Ryan closed his notebook. "Mind if I walk with you?"

She hesitated again, then nodded. "Sure."

As they stepped out into the cool evening, Layla glanced sideways at him. He didn't feel like someone she had just met. And somehow, she had a feeling he'd be around again.

The book was heavy in her bag. And she was starting to suspect that picking it up had been the easiest part.

# IV
## Between the lines

Layla had read the same paragraph four times and still didn't understand it. Not because it was difficult, but because it wasn't there yesterday.

The page in the book—the book—had changed again.

Her own thoughts were on the paper. Her hesitation about Ryan. Her late-night pacing. The moment she almost told Ana about the whispering pages but didn't.

The book knew.

She snapped it shut and pushed it under her pillow just as Ayaan burst in, Nerf gun in hand. "Laylaaaa! I got you this time!"

"You literally didn't," she muttered, dodging the foam dart.

He grinned and plopped onto her bed. "What's under the pillow?"

"None of your business."

"Ooooh, secrets," he teased.

Layla shoved him off with a smile and chased him out of her room. It was the first time in days she felt like herself.

---

Later, at school

Mr. Nathaniel Bennett stood at the front of the classroom, reciting lines from a poem with theatrical flair. "And all the world began to burn, though no one lit the flame…"

Ana leaned over. "That guy definitely practices in front of a mirror."

Layla smiled faintly.

"You still haven't told me what was in that book."

"Still figuring it out," Layla said.

Ana narrowed her eyes. "You sure you're okay?"

"I'm fine," Layla lied.

---

After school , at The Lantern

Layla hadn't planned to go back to the Lantern so soon. But something pulled her there—curiosity, fear, maybe something else. Mr. Williams was at the desk, sorting through old donation boxes.

He looked up and smiled. "Back again, Miss Singh."

"Hi," she said. "I just… wanted some quiet."

"Quiet is all we have here," he replied with a dry chuckle.

Layla hesitated, then asked, "Do you remember that black book? The one I found a few days ago?"

Mr. Williams frowned. "black book?"

"It was… on the back shelves. Old, no title."

He scratched his beard. "I don't recall putting out anything like that."

"But I—" She stopped. "Never mind."

He gave her a curious look but said nothing more.

Layla sat down at her regular spot, same corner as before.

She opened the book again, holding her breath.

More words.

*"" The boy with the patient eyes knows more than he lets on.""*
Layla blinked.

Ryan?

She flipped the page. Ink spread across it like oil blooming on water. New words formed—right in front of her.

She was being watched.

Her head snapped up.

Nothing.

But the feeling remained, crawling across her skin like cold wind.

She packed up and left quickly, not looking back.

---

Evening, at Home

Dinner was a loud, chaotic blend of overlapping voices, sizzling parathas, and the comforting scent of turmeric and fried onions.

Ayaan was mid-story, waving a spoon in the air like a sword. "Then Jay dared me to climb the monkey bars backwards. I almost made it—but then this squirrel came out of nowhere—"

Mrs. Singh gasped. "A squirrel?"

"He's exaggerating," Layla said, grinning.

Mr. Singh chuckled. "Even so, I respect the squirrel. Sounds like he saved you from falling."

"I didn't fall. I jumped off."

"You scraped your elbow," Layla pointed out.

"Battle scars," Ayaan said proudly.

Their mom shook her head, reaching over to tuck his hair behind his ear. "You're lucky you didn't break something. And Layla—you're too quiet these days."

"I'm just tired," Layla said, forcing a smile. "We have a lot of reading in literature class."

Her dad passed the bowl of dal to her. "Beta, don't push yourself too hard. You already take everything so seriously."

"I know," she murmured, filling her plate even though she wasn't hungry.

Later, the family sat together on the couch, a Bollywood movie playing in the background. Ayaan dozed off with his head in her lap, and her mom braided the ends of Layla's hair absentmindedly.

Layla let her eyes close just for a second.

For a moment, everything felt normal.

But somewhere under her bed, the book waited.

And it was never done writing.

# V
# Parallels And Glitches

Layla couldn't shake the feeling that something was off. It wasn't just the oddities in the book she had discovered—no, it was deeper than that. The world around her seemed to be shifting ever so slightly, as if someone had nudged reality out of alignment and she was the only one who noticed.

Her morning had started like any other. Ayaan had barged into her room, demanding she watch a video of a cat doing backflips. Her mother had offered the usual "eat more, beta" as Layla pushed around her breakfast. But as the day went on, small inconsistencies began to pop up.

At school, Layla sat beside Ana in Literature class, as she always did. Ana was scribbling in her notebook again, her pen flying across the pages in a blur of motion. But today, Layla couldn't help but notice something strange—Ana's sketches had changed.

The sketchbook was still full of portraits—faces, different expressions—but today, the faces felt... wrong. The eyes were too wide, the smiles too sharp, as though they were more like masks than real people. Layla tried to ignore it, but something about them unsettled her.

"What's up?" Ana asked, catching Layla staring. "You look like you're a million miles away."

Layla blinked, forcing a smile. "Just thinking."

Ana raised an eyebrow, clearly unconvinced, but she didn't press it. "You should come by after school. I need your opinion on something. I was playing around with double exposures, and I think I might've captured something... weird."

Layla nodded, though the idea of seeing more oddities—more things that didn't feel right—made her heart race. Still, she couldn't back out. Ana was her closest friend, and she needed to talk to someone. Maybe it was all in her head.

---

Later that afternoon, Layla stood in Ana's room, watching as Ana fiddled with her camera. The room was familiar—sunlight filtering through the blinds, casting long shadows across the floor, posters of old film stars decorating the walls. But there was something about the quietness that felt wrong.

Ana had already started flipping through the photos on her camera's display. She swiped at the first image.

"Here it is," Ana said, pointing to a black-and-white photo of a tree with distorted branches. "See how it looks... different? It's like the branches don't align right."

Layla squinted at the photo. The branches did seem odd, bending in impossible angles, as if the tree had been pulled out of reality and shoved back in wrong.

"Maybe it's just a trick of the light," Layla suggested, though her voice lacked conviction.

Ana shook her head. "No way. Look at this one." She flipped to the next photo. This time, it was a simple shot of the school courtyard—a crowd of students walking, some laughing, some talking in groups. Layla recognized a few faces from her class.

But one of them—an older student she didn't know—was staring directly at the camera. It was an unsettling stare, as though he was looking straight at Layla, his eyes so sharp that it felt as if they were digging into her skin.

"That's... not right," Layla said, her voice barely above a whisper.

"I know, right? I didn't notice it when I took the picture," Ana replied, her tone more serious now. "I don't even remember seeing him in the courtyard when I was shooting."

Layla's heart skipped a beat. "That's... creepy. Could it be a glitch in your camera?"

"I don't think so. I've checked the settings like ten times. Nothing's off."

Layla felt a sudden tightness in her chest. She stood up, pacing the room, her mind racing.

"Maybe you should stop taking photos for a while," Layla suggested, her voice tight. "There's something... off about them."

Ana shot her a confused look. "Stop? Why?"

"Because it feels like it's—" Layla paused, trying to find the right words. "Like it's catching things that aren't supposed to be there."

Before Ana could respond, Layla's phone buzzed in her pocket. She pulled it out, her fingers trembling slightly as she read the message.

Mom: We're having dinner early tonight. Don't be late!

Layla frowned. Dinner? It was only 6:30.

"I need to go," Layla said quickly. "My parents are... well, they want me home early for some reason."

Ana looked at her, still holding the camera in her hands, but didn't argue. She nodded, though her expression remained puzzled. "I'll text you later about the photos."

"Sure," Layla said, her mind already elsewhere.

---

When Layla arrived home, she found her parents sitting at the dining table, the food already served, and the atmosphere unusually tense. Ayaan was nowhere to be found.

"Where's Ayaan?" Layla asked as she took a seat.

"He's out with his friends," her mom replied, her voice soft but sharp, as though she were trying to mask something.

Layla froze mid-reach. "What? He was grounded."

Mrs. Singh's hand paused in midair, but only for a second. "Grounded? What for?"

"The window. He shattered it playing cricket in the hallway two days ago."

Mr. Singh laughed softly. "You must be confusing things, Layla. That happened when he was eight. In our old house."

"No," she said, sitting up straighter. "It was this week. You yelled. You said no screens, no outside, one week minimum."

Her mother's brow furrowed—but not in concern. In confusion, maybe pity. "Layla... we never said that. Ayaan hasn't broken anything lately. Are you feeling okay, beta?"

Layla opened her mouth, then shut it. The air in the room felt heavier now, thicker. She looked at the sideboard where Ayaan's school photo usually sat. It was gone. Or maybe... had it ever been there?

She glanced back at them. They were still eating. Calm. Chatting about some office thing, about someone's retirement party.

Was she the only one who remembered?

She slowly filled her plate, appetite gone.

Later, after the meal, the family gathered in the living room like usual. A movie played—some comedy her mom loved—but the sound felt far away. Layla sat on the edge of the couch, rethinking the details her family recalls differently.

Her parents didn't seem to notice anything off. Her mother even laughed at a joke on screen, the sound too loud, too normal.

---

Later that night, Layla lay in her bed, the book under her pillow, its pages whispering to her. She had been avoiding it, but now, she could feel it calling to her, demanding her attention.

She pulled the book out and opened it.

The words were already there.

*"The girl remembers her brother being grounded for a week, but it never happened"*

Her fingers shook as she read the line again, and then again.

She was being rewritten. Her memories were not her own. And the book—it knew everything.

# VI
## Echoing In The Pages

The Lantern seemed colder than usual that afternoon. Layla had wandered through its aisles for hours, the silence wrapping around her like a heavy blanket. The smell of old paper and dust was comforting, but today, it felt more like a trap, as if the walls were whispering secrets she wasn't ready to hear.

The book was still with her, tucked under her arm, its presence growing heavier with every minute. She had to know what it said. She had to understand why the words were changing—why they felt so... personal.

She sat at one of the small tables near the back, eyes fixed on the pages, but it was as if the ink kept shifting, like the words were slipping through her fingers, refusing to stay still.

*"" She felt the eyes of the town on her. The fog was closing in, thickening around the streets. She turned*

*the corner, passing the place where she had once walked with him. The shadows seemed to stretch longer now, but they were familiar.""*

Layla's breath caught. The passage mirrored exactly where she had been earlier that morning, walking through the fog on her way to the library. It felt too real—like the book was seeing her, tracking her every move. She slammed it shut, heart racing.

The library felt even emptier now, the air thick with tension. She didn't know how long she had been sitting there, but when she stood up, the room seemed to tilt, as if the ground beneath her was shifting with every step.

With a quick glance around, Layla slipped the book back into her bag and made her way to the door. The bell above it jingled softly as she stepped into the cool air, the thick fog still hanging heavily in the streets of Maplewood. It was quiet—too quiet. Layla pulled her coat tighter around her, the fog clinging to her skin like an unshakable presence.

As she stepped out into the soft light of late afternoon, Maplewood greeted her with the scent of lilacs and the sound of distant lawnmowers. Her boots clicked on the sidewalk as she passed rows of pastel houses, each with picket fences and flower beds.

"Hey."

Layla turned.

Ryan stood a few paces behind her, hands in his hoodie pockets, his hair tousled like he'd just come from a nap—or a daydream. He looked more awake than usual, his eyes catching the sun in a way that made them seem lighter.

"Hey," she said, surprised but not unhappy to see him.

He fell into step beside her.

"You live this way too?" she asked.

"Nope," he said. "But I saw you come out of the library. Thought maybe you could use a walking buddy."

She raised an eyebrow. "Do I look like I need one?"

"Everyone does sometimes."

They walked in silence for a moment. The kind that didn't press. The good kind.

"So," he said eventually, "if you had to eat one food for the rest of your life—just one—what would it be?"

Layla laughed. "That's random."

"It's serious. Your entire happiness could depend on this answer."

She pretended to think hard. "Okay. Aloo paratha. With butter."

He grinned. "Respect."

"What about you?"

"Easy. Grilled cheese. With tomato soup. No contest."

They turned onto Oak Lane, where the trees arched overhead like an invitation.

"What were you doing at the library?" Ryan asked.

"Just reading. Escaping a bit."

"Same."

"You don't even go there that much."

"I said escaping. Didn't say where from."

That hung between them for a beat.

Layla looked at him sideways. "You're kind of mysterious, you know."

"People say that when they don't know what box to put someone in."

She nodded. "I get that."

They passed Maplewood Park. A group of kids were tossing a frisbee near the pond, and someone was playing guitar under a tree. The sun was about to set and the shared experience of watching the sunset, the colors mirroring the warmth in their hearts, felt like a silent vow

"Do you ever think about leaving?" Layla asked suddenly. "This town, I mean."

"Every day."

She smiled. "Same."

"But I also kind of love it," he added. "Hate it and love it. Like family."

Layla looked up at the soft clouds overhead, drifting like lazy thoughts. "Sometimes I feel like Maplewood is holding its breath. Like it's waiting for something."

Ryan tilted his head. "What do you think it's waiting for?"

"I don't know," she said. "A change? Or maybe just someone to notice it."

He glanced at her, and for a second, the air shifted. Something almost unspoken passed between them.

"Want to keep walking?" he asked.

She nodded. "Sure."

They walked past the bakery where the windows always fogged up and the smell of cinnamon wafted out like a spell. Past old Mrs. Delaney's porch with the wind chimes that sounded like glass laughter. Down toward the winding edge of the neighborhood, where the houses got bigger and further apart.

They talked about music. About how she hated mornings and he wrote best when he couldn't sleep. About Ana's obsession with photographing clouds and how Layla once tried to dye her hair purple in eighth grade and ended up with lilac streaks for a month.

Ryan told her about his older brother, who lived in Portland, and how sometimes he left notes around the house just to make people smile. Layla told him about the time Ayaan tried to set up a lemonade stand in winter because "snow lemonade" sounded like a good idea.

By the time they looped back toward Layla's street, it was dusk. The sky blushed orange and pink, and streetlamps flickered on one by one.

Ryan kicked at a pebble on the sidewalk. "So... if I asked you to walk again next week, would you say yes?"

Layla's lips tugged into a soft smile. "I might."

He nodded. "Cool."

They reached her gate. She paused, hand on the latch.

"Thanks for the walk," she said.

"Anytime," he replied.

She watched him walk a few steps, then turn back and flash a grin. "Also—aloo paratha? Solid choice."

She laughed, the sound catching in the warm evening air.

Inside, the house smelled like masala and comfort. Ayaan was yelling about something on TV. Her parents were arguing over the right amount of ginger to use in chai.

Everything felt normal.

But Layla's heartbeat wasn't.

Because for the first time in a while, she wasn't thinking about the book.

She was thinking about Ryan.

# VII

# Shadows And Light

The corner café in Maplewood smelled like cinnamon and stories—old furniture, mismatched mugs, and the hum of quiet conversations. Layla stirred the whipped cream into her hot chocolate while Ana sat across from her, camera resting on the table between them.

"It's too pretty today to stay inside," Ana said, already angling her phone to catch a golden beam of sunlight streaming through the window. "We should walk after this. The light is perfect for portraits."

"You always say that," Layla said with a smile.

"Because it's always true," Ana replied. "And you, my friend, are a very underappreciated muse."

Layla rolled her eyes. "You just like bossing me around."

Ana grinned. "Only a little."

Outside the window, Maplewood moved slowly—people strolling, leaving dancing in the breeze, and the occasional bark of a dog echoing down the street. Ana leaned back in her chair and snapped a photo of Layla mid-sip.

"No warning?"

"It's candid! That's how I get the magic."

Layla shook her head but didn't protest.

They talked about random things—school, Mrs. Bennet's obsession with Shakespeare, a new indie band Ana liked. It was easy and comfortable.

Then Ana said, "Okay, last one," and lifted her camera again.

Layla posed jokingly, chin raised dramatically. Ana laughed and clicked the shutter. She glanced at the screen, then frowned.

"What?" Layla asked.

Ana's eyebrows drew together. "That's weird. The mirror behind you—"

Layla turned. The café wall had an antique mirror, slightly spotted with age. It reflected the room perfectly—empty tables, the counter, the door—

But not Layla.

Layla was missing.

Ana slowly turned the camera toward her again, snapped another picture, and looked.

Still no reflection.

"Is it the angle?" Ana muttered, lifting her phone and snapping a shot with it too.

Same result.

Layla leaned over. "Let me see."

Ana hesitated, then showed her the photo.

Layla stared at it. Her figure was clear. But in the mirror behind her, there was only the empty chair.

Her stomach dropped. "Okay... that's... weird."

Ana glanced at her. "Layla?"

"I'm fine," Layla said quickly, standing. "Let's go walk. You were right—the light's good."

Ana looked like she wanted to push further, but she didn't. She just slung her camera over her shoulder and stood.

As they left the café, Layla didn't look back at the mirror. Because she wasn't sure what she'd see if she did.

The sidewalks of Maplewood gleamed in the late afternoon sun. Trees whispered overhead, their new leaves flickering green and gold. Layla and Ana walked side by side, the quiet rhythm of their steps a contrast to the unease twisting low in Layla's stomach.

Ana's camera swung lightly from her shoulder, but she hadn't raised it again. Not since the mirror.

"You okay?" she asked finally.

Layla kicked a pebble on the path. "Yeah. Just tired, maybe. That photo—it's probably just a trick of the light. Old mirrors are weird."

Ana didn't answer for a moment. "Yeah. Probably."

They passed a florist setting out pots of marigolds and roses, their colors almost violently bright in the sun.

"I'm thinking of submitting something to the Maplewood Photo Contest," Ana said, like she'd flipped an inner switch. "Something eerie. Not like the usual golden-hour stuff. Shadows. Ghost-town vibes. Think that'd stand out?"

Layla smiled, relieved at the change in topic. "You'd win."

"I mean, maybe. If my camera stops acting possessed."

"You've always said it has a mind of its own."

Ana grinned. "It's definitely got an attitude."

They turned onto one of Maplewood's narrower lanes—lined with old brownstones and wrought-iron fences. The world was quieter here. Even the birdsong felt distant.

Layla glanced at a window they passed and caught Ana 's reflection in the glass. Just Ana 's. Not hers.

She blinked, turned— Ana was right there, walking close, talking about shadows and sepia tones. Layla didn't say anything.

Not yet.

They reached a small park tucked between the streets. It had one crooked bench and a rusted swing set that squeaked when the wind caught it.

"I used to come here when I was little," Layla said, sitting on the bench. "Pretending the swings could take me somewhere else."

Ana sat beside her. "Where would you go?"

"Somewhere quiet. Somewhere... outside everything."

Ana nudged her shoulder. "You're already kind of outside everything, you know. Always dreaming. Always reading."

Layla gave a small laugh. "Maybe I like it there."

"I know you do. But I like you here."

They sat in companionable silence for a while, the kind only close friends can share.

Then Ana added softly, "Just don't disappear on me, okay?"

Layla turned toward her. "What?"

"Lately, you've seemed... I don't know. Slippery. Like I blink and you're someone else."

Layla looked down at her hands.

"I'm still me," she said.

But even as she said it, she wasn't sure it was true.

They talked about regulars—school, photography, books , and many more.

A half-broken basketball court stretched behind the swings, where a boy in a grey hoodie dribbled a faded ball. His movements were smooth, practiced—like muscle memory. Even from a distance, Layla knew it was him.

Ryan Cole.

He noticed them almost instantly. Paused mid-dribble, gave a single wave.

"Hey," he called, not loud but clear.

"Hey," Layla replied automatically, her voice catching in her throat.

Then he turned back to the hoop, launched a clean shot, and kept playing—just as quietly as before. No invitation. No conversation. Just acknowledgment.

Ana raised an eyebrow. "So that's him?"

Layla tried to play dumb. "Him who?"

"Don't even. Ryan Cole. The mysterious boy you keep running into like it's fate or something."

"It's not fate."

"Mmm." Ana leaned back on the bench. "You like him?"

Layla hesitated.

Ana smirked. "That's a yes."

"I don't know," Layla said, kicking at the dirt. "He's... different."

"You say that like it's a bad thing."

"It's not. I just... I don't know what it is yet."

Ana gave her a knowing look. "You don't need to know. You just need to notice how you feel when he's around."

Layla didn't reply, but her heart did a little flip.

On the court, Ryan took another shot. Swish. No look. No celebration.

Just a quiet presence.

And then, just as the sun was beginning to dip, Layla felt it. A twinge at the back of her mind, like a whisper too faint to hear, but enough to make her pulse quicken.

The book. The one still tucked beneath her bag, patiently waiting. Its presence had never fully left her—like an itch that refused to be scratched. It wasn't just the words that unnerved her. It was the way the world around her seemed to blur and shift, moments lingering longer than they should.

Layla glanced back at Ryan, who was now pulling off his hoodie and throwing it over a nearby bench, preparing to shoot again.

Everything seemed... normal.

But there was that feeling again. The book, waiting for her. Watching her. Ready to change everything.

# VIII
## The Pages Between US

The next day, Layla woke up to the taste of sandpaper in her throat and a heaviness behind her eyes. Her alarm had been going off for the past five minutes, its shrill beeping slicing through the fog of her sleep.

From downstairs, she could already hear the morning chaos—pots clinking, Ayaan's voice rising in protest, the kettle whistling like it was losing its mind.

Her door creaked open.

"Layla?" Her mother's voice was soft but alert. "You're not up?"

"I don't feel good," Layla mumbled.

Her mom stepped in, brushing a hand against Layla's forehead. "You're a little warm. Throat?"

"Sore," she said, wincing.

"Hmm," her mom said, already heading toward the dresser. "No school for you today. I'll call in."

Layla blinked at her. "You're not going to argue first?"

"You don't look like you're faking," her mom said, handing her a glass of warm water. "And you haven't skipped a day since school started. Rest. I'll leave some khichdi in the fridge."

Layla managed a faint smile. "Thanks, Ma."

As her mom turned to go, she paused at the door. "And no sneaking off to the Lantern today, okay?"

Layla looked away. "I wasn't going to."

Her mother gave her a knowing look, then disappeared down the hallway.

Left alone, Layla stared at the ceiling. The dream was already fading from memory, but she remembered the last part clearly: she had been inside the book again, running—always running—while the words crumbled off the pages like ash. No matter how fast she went, something stayed right behind her.

The morning passed in a blur of half-sleep, tea, and dull television noise. Layla could hear her mom bustling around the house, making phone calls, the occasional sound of Ayaan's laughter echoing from the kitchen. But for the most part, the day felt like it was moving around her, too fast, too distant. She couldn't concentrate on anything, not even the words in the book she'd left hidden under her pillow.

By the time the sun was high enough to send streams of golden light into her room, Layla felt restless. The soreness in her throat hadn't eased, but her body, heavy with lethargy, longed to be out of bed, to stretch her legs, to breathe fresh air.

She pulled on a sweatshirt and some jeans, hoping the cool breeze outside would clear her foggy head. The thought of the Lantern made her hesitant—she was still drawn to the place, but her mom's warning echoed in her mind.

Still, the pull was too strong. She slipped out of the house quietly, not wanting to wake anyone up further.

---

The streets of Maplewood were quieter than usual, the late morning light filtering through the trees, casting soft shadows along the sidewalk. Layla didn't know exactly why she was walking toward The Lantern again. She had only just left her house after spending most of the morning resting, nursing a sore throat and feeling a general sense of fatigue. But the pull of the library was undeniable.

There was something about the quiet, the smell of old pages and dust, the constant feeling of being surrounded by stories and worlds untold. It had become a refuge for her in the past few days, and she found herself wandering there more than she intended. Maybe it was the need for silence. Maybe it was to avoid the whirling thoughts in her head, constantly swirling around the book, the changes she felt in her life, the feeling that things weren't quite as they seemed.

As she neared the library, she felt the cool breeze ruffle her hair, the soreness in her throat making her wince slightly with each breath. She wasn't feeling 100%—but then again, she hadn't been for a while. She pushed open the door to the library, the familiar scent of old books welcoming her inside. It was dimmer than usual, and the only sounds were the soft shuffle of pages and the quiet murmur of Mr. Williams at the front desk.

She walked slowly through the aisles, her eyes scanning the shelves but not really seeing anything in particular. Her mind was elsewhere, focused on the strange feeling that had followed her the last few days—the sensation of things shifting around her, of her life being written or rewritten by some unseen hand.

As she turned the corner toward the back of the library, she froze. There, leaning against the bookshelf near her favorite spot, was Ryan.

He didn't see her immediately. His head was bent, focused on a book in his hands. Layla felt a strange flutter in her chest, a mixture of surprise and something else she couldn't quite place. She hadn't expected to see him here. In fact, she hadn't even considered it as a possibility. But there he was, in the place she often retreated to for solace, with his eyes deeply absorbed in the pages in front of him.

The sound of her footsteps must have alerted him. He looked up, a soft, easy smile spreading across his face when he saw her.

"Hey," he said, his voice warm and inviting.

Layla felt herself smile back, even though she wasn't entirely sure what to say. She had to admit, seeing him here was unexpected, but somehow it didn't feel as awkward as it probably should have. It felt... natural.

"Hey," Layla replied, her voice softer than she intended. She cleared her throat, still feeling the remnants of her sore throat but trying to push through it. "I didn't expect to see you here."

Ryan chuckled, his eyes crinkling at the corners. "Yeah, I've kind of been on a reading kick lately. Been coming in here whenever I get the chance."

"Same," Layla said, feeling a little more at ease. "I guess there's something about this place that makes everything else fade away. Like nothing else matters here."

He nodded, closing the book in his hands and resting it on the table next to him. "Exactly. It's like you can just get lost in here. The whole world disappears for a while."

For a moment, they stood there, the silence between them comfortable. Ryan shifted slightly, his gaze drifting to the shelves around them.

"You come here often?" Layla asked, genuinely curious.

"Yeah, a lot actually," he said, running a hand through his hair. "I like the older sections. You know, the ones with all the dusty books that haven't been touched in years."

Layla smiled, a bit of laughter escaping her. "Sounds like you're a fan of the… forgotten books."

Ryan shrugged. "Something like that. They've got character, you know? They've been here longer than us, and they've still got stories to tell."

Layla couldn't help but think of the black book she had found, the one that had started all of this, and the way it seemed to have its own stories to tell. She pushed the thought aside, not wanting to bring up the mysterious book to Ryan just yet.

"Well," she said, shifting the conversation, "I guess I'm just here to get away from… everything. It's been a weird couple of days."

Ryan's eyes softened, a hint of concern flashing in them. "Weird how?"

She hesitated, not sure how to explain the strange, creeping feeling that had taken hold of her life. The way things seemed off, like they were shifting out of place.

"It's just… I don't know," she said finally, her voice quiet. "Things feel different. Like I'm… not fully in control, or something. Like things around me are changing without me even realizing it."

Ryan didn't speak right away. He studied her, a thoughtful expression on his face. Finally, he spoke. "I know what you mean. I've felt that way before—like everything's slipping away, and you can't catch it. But, you know, sometimes it's good to let go. To just… let things be, even if you can't control them."

Layla stared at him, surprised by his insight. There was something in the way he spoke, like he had experienced that same feeling before. Like he understood exactly what she was going through.

"I guess so," Layla said, her voice barely above a whisper. She wasn't sure what to say next, or how to explain the strange feeling that had become a constant presence in her life.

Ryan seemed to sense her unease, because he smiled, breaking the tension. "I get it, Layla. Trust me, I do. But hey, sometimes it's okay not to have all the answers. It's okay to just... be for a while."

His words were simple, but they carried a weight that settled over her, making her feel less alone. She smiled back, grateful for his understanding, even if she didn't have all the answers yet.

"Thanks, Ryan," she said quietly.

"Anytime," he replied, his smile was genuine. "I'm here whenever you need a distraction, or just someone to talk to."

Layla nodded, feeling a small sense of relief. Maybe it wasn't the answers she needed—maybe it was just someone to listen to, someone who understood the weight of the world she was carrying without needing an explanation. She was starting to realize that Ryan wasn't just a guy she occasionally bumped into at school. He was someone who might just become a steady presence in her life.

For a moment, the world outside seemed to fade away as she stood there in the library, the quiet hum of the space around them, the soft rustle of pages and distant footsteps. And for the first time in days, Layla felt like she could breathe a little easier.

Layla stood there for a moment, her mind still processing the warmth of their conversation. It was surprising how much easier it had been to talk to Ryan than she had anticipated. It felt like they'd stepped into a space between them that was only theirs, a comfortable silence that existed without pressure. She wasn't sure why, but she found herself wanting to stay in this moment, wanting to feel the simple relief of just... being.

Ryan stood up and stretched, breaking the quiet. "Want to take a walk?" he asked, his tone light but with a sense of something deeper beneath it.

Layla glanced around. It was a perfect day outside, the sun shining through the trees outside the library, the air warm but not too hot. Her mind briefly flickered to the ache in her throat, but she dismissed it. She'd be fine for now.

"Sure," she said, offering him a soft smile.

They walked outside together, side by side, not saying much at first. The streets of Maplewood were quiet in the early afternoon, the sidewalks dappled with the shadow of trees. Layla noticed how peaceful the town felt today, as though it was in a moment of suspension, waiting for something to happen. And perhaps it was—she just wasn't sure what that something was.

As they walked, Layla couldn't help but admire the ease with which Ryan moved through the world. His casual stride, the way his hair was tousled just enough to give him a carefree look, the way he seemed to absorb everything around him—everything about him felt... natural, almost magnetic.

Ryan was talking about a movie he had watched recently, something about a spy thriller. Layla found herself half-listening, half-watching him, her gaze shifting from his expressive face to his hands as they gestured with his words. There was something about him that made her heart beat a little faster, something she couldn't quite place. Maybe it was the way he listened, or the way he smiled like he knew something more than he was letting on.

She liked that. She liked that about him.

"Are you even listening to me?" Ryan's voice broke through her thoughts, teasing but also laced with curiosity.

Layla blinked, her cheeks flushing slightly. "Sorry, I... was distracted."

Ryan raised an eyebrow but smiled. "What's going on in that head of yours?"

Layla hesitated, unsure whether she should tell him what she was thinking. How she'd been feeling a little overwhelmed lately, how his presence in the library had felt like a small spark in a dark room. But instead, she shrugged.

"Just thinking," she said, offering him a small smile.

Ryan seemed to accept that. They continued walking, turning a corner and heading toward the park. The streets were still quiet, the occasional passerby greeting them with a friendly nod. The late afternoon light filtered through the trees, casting long, soft shadows across the sidewalk. Layla couldn't help but notice the beauty of it—the way the world looked more vibrant, almost magical, in Ryan's presence.

They reached the park, and for the first time, Layla realized how much she had been looking forward to this walk with him. She had been too distracted by the book, by the strange happenings in her life, that she hadn't allowed herself the luxury of enjoying the moment. Now, walking beside Ryan in the peacefulness of the afternoon, she realized just how much she wanted to stay in this feeling, this simple sense of connection.

They stopped at a bench near the edge of the park, overlooking the small pond where ducks paddled lazily in the water. Ryan sat down first, and Layla followed suit, her gaze lingering on the ducks for a moment before turning back to him.

Ryan was quiet for a moment, his gaze fixed on the pond, but his body was turned slightly toward her. He seemed to be gathering his thoughts, and Layla could sense that something was about to change.

After a few moments, Ryan shifted, his eyes meeting hers. There was a vulnerability in his expression, something that made Layla's heart skip a beat.

"Layla," he began, his voice low but steady. "There's something I've been wanting to tell you. Something I don't really know how to say, but I think you deserve to hear it."

Layla's pulse quickened, and she could feel a wave of anticipation building in her chest. She swallowed, her throat still sore but her mind racing with possibilities. Was he about to say something important? Something she wasn't ready for?

Ryan took a breath, his eyes locking with hers. "I know we've only known each other for a little while, and I don't know if this is crazy or not, but... I like you. I really do. More than I thought I would."

Layla froze. Her heart thudded in her chest, the words hanging in the air between them like a fragile thing.

"I like you too," she said quietly, her voice barely a whisper. It was true. She had felt it—the way she felt drawn to him, the way he made her feel like she could just be herself without pretense.

Ryan smiled, the relief evident in his expression. He shifted a little closer, his eyes never leaving hers. "I don't know what this is between us yet, but I want to see where it goes. I want to spend more time with you. And, well... I guess I'm asking you, Layla, if you'd be open to that. To seeing where this could go."

Layla felt her heart flutter in her chest, the moment surreal. She hadn't expected this—she hadn't expected him to say it so openly, so earnestly. But she also realized that, in a way, she had been hoping for this. Hoping that this connection between them was real, that it wasn't just her imagination, that he felt it too.

"I'd like that," she said, her voice steady now, a warmth spreading through her chest. "I'd like that very much."

Ryan's face lit up with a smile, and for a moment, everything felt perfect. The quiet of the park, the soft rustle of leaves, the distant sound of children playing—everything seemed to fade away, leaving just the two of them, sitting there, together.

"I'm glad," Ryan said softly, his hand brushing against hers on the bench.

Layla's breath caught at the small touch, the spark of connection between them igniting into something deeper. She let herself relax into the moment, the worry and the uncertainty about everything else in her life slipping away.

For the first time in days, everything felt.... right.

# IX
# What You Choose To Read

The halls of Riverstone High hummed with typical weekday chaos—laughter echoing off lockers, sneakers squeaking on tile, the rustle of paper and chatter. Layla felt strangely grounded in it all. For the first time in weeks, things felt... normal.

The cafeteria buzzed with noise—clinking trays, bursts of laughter, the occasional shout across a table. Layla stood in line with Ana, tray in hand, while Ryan waited at their usual corner table by the windows.

"So," Ana said, eyeing the mashed potatoes suspiciously. "What's the vibe today? Is it edible?"

Layla smiled, distracted. "I mean, barely. But I guess we will survive."

They paid for their food and headed over to Ryan. He looked up as they approached, moving his backpack off the bench.

"Ladies," he said, a playful nod. "The culinary excellence of Riverstone High awaits."

"You joke," Ana said, sliding into the seat across from him, "but this pasta could double as glue."

Ryan glanced at Layla. "I brought snacks. Emergency rations."

"You're a hero," Layla said with a small laugh, settling next to him.

There was something new between them—nothing dramatic, but subtle. The way Ryan's shoulder brushed hers, and she didn't move away. The way Layla smiled just a bit longer. Ana raised an eyebrow.

"Alright," she said, tearing open a juice box. "Spill."

"Spill what?" Layla asked, stabbing at her pasta.

"That smile. The weird not-smile. The... vibe."

Ryan raised an eyebrow. "The vibe?"

Ana waved her fork between the two of them. "Yes, the vibe. This is new. Don't pretend it's not."

Layla hesitated, then glanced at Ryan. He gave her a little nod, like, Go ahead.

"We're... kind of seeing each other," she said, suddenly very interested in her applesauce.

Ana's eyes widened. "You're kidding."

Layla peeked at her. "Nope."

Ana slammed her juice box on the table—dramatically, but still managed not to spill anything. "Oh my god. Finally."

Layla blinked. "Finally?"

"Please," Ana said, leaning in. "I've been waiting for this to happen since like... the first time you mentioned how 'quiet and mysterious' he was."

Ryan chuckled, glancing down at his tray. "Was that how you described me?"

Layla blushed. "Maybe."

Ana grinned. "This is so cute I might throw up."

"Please don't," Ryan said. "Not while we're eating."

Ana rolled her eyes, then softened. "I'm happy for you guys. You seem... really good together."

"We are," Layla said, and this time she didn't hide the smile.

They moved on to lighter things—memes, weekend plans, Mr. Bennett's dramatic poetry reading from earlier that morning. At one point, Ana tried to do an impression of his voice, sending all three of them into a fit of giggles that earned a few glances from nearby tables.

Layla leaned back, watching her best friend and her boyfriend laugh across the table, and felt something she hadn't felt in a while—ease.

The book didn't press at the back of her mind. Not here. Not right now.

---

The final bell rang, its echo lingering in the air like the last note of a song. Students surged through the corridors of Riverstone High, their voices overlapping in a familiar end-of-day hum.

Layla walked beside Ana and Ryan, the spring sun casting a soft, golden glow over the front courtyard. The breeze carried the scent of budding flowers and warm pavement, a reminder that Maplewood's long winter was truly over.

Ryan adjusted the strap of his gym bag and sighed. "Basketball practice awaits."

Ana rolled her eyes. "Try not to wipe out again, superstar."

"That was not my fault," Ryan protested. "I was sabotaged by a very aggressive water bottle."

Layla laughed, the sound quiet but real. "Sure, sure. Go show them how it's done."

Ryan paused just outside the school gate. "I'll see you later, yeah?"

"Yeah," she said, tucking a strand of hair behind her ear.

He stepped closer, brushing his fingers gently along her hand as if asking permission. Then, with a soft smile, he leaned in and pressed a kiss to her forehead.

It wasn't rushed or awkward. It was warm, steady, and full of unspoken care.

Layla's breath hitched. The world seemed to still for a second—the sounds around her dimmed, and all she could focus on was the quiet thud of her heart.

Ryan pulled back slowly, eyes still on her. "Take care, okay?"

Layla nodded, her cheeks flushed with a color she couldn't hide. "You too."

He grinned, eyes flicking to Ana. "Don't let her bully you."

"Me?" Ana gasped. "I'm a ray of sunshine."

Ryan jogged off toward the gym, waving over his shoulder.

Ana turned to Layla with wide eyes. "Did you see that? Did I see that? That was, like... so cute I might explode."

Layla let out a breath she hadn't realized she was holding. "I—yeah."

Her fingers ghosted over the spot on her forehead where his lips had touched. It was such a simple gesture, yet it left her skin tingling and her heart fluttering like it was learning how to fly.

"Okay, I'm officially shipping you two," Ana said. "Name ideas? Rayla? Layan?"

Layla laughed, shaking her head. "You're impossible."

They reached the sidewalk and paused at the fork in the road—one way toward downtown's bustling café row, the other leading to the quiet streets that wound toward the Lantern.

"You coming with me?" Ana asked.

"I think I'll head to the library," Layla said. "Just for a little while."

Ana tilted her head knowingly. "Of course. You and your dusty old books."

Layla smiled. "They're reliable."

Ana smirked. "Unlike certain sweaty basketball boys?"

Layla rolled her eyes, but her smile didn't fade.

"Alright, enjoy the quiet. Text me when you're done being mysterious and brooding."

"I will," Layla promised.

As Ana disappeared down the street, Layla turned toward the familiar path to The Lantern, her hand still unconsciously brushing her forehead, a quiet joy blooming in her chest.

---

The streets of Maplewood were quieter now, the late afternoon sun casting long shadows on the sidewalk. Layla walked slowly, letting her thoughts drift. Every step seemed to echo with the memory of Ryan's touch—a simple forehead kiss, yet it still warmed her like a hidden ember.

She reached The Lantern just as the golden light spilled through its tall windows, stretching across the hardwood floor like fingers reaching for stories.

The bell over the door jingled.

Mr. Williams looked up from behind the counter, adjusting his reading glasses. "Miss Singh. Twice in one week? At this rate, I'll have to put you on payroll."

Layla smiled faintly. "I could reshelve the horror section."

He chuckled. "No one wants to touch the horror section."

Layla glanced around the familiar space. It smelled of paper, wood polish, and the faint citrusy scent of old ink. Her feet led her upstairs before she even had to think about it—toward the same corner she always gravitated to now.

The black book was waiting, just as she'd left it. But she hesitated.

Instead of sitting, she walked over to the railing, gazing down at the rows of shelves below. Something felt off. Not wrong, exactly—just... tense. Like the pages were holding their breath.

She didn't even notice Mr. Williams had followed her until he spoke.

"You're not just here for quiet, are you?"

Layla turned, startled. "What do you mean?"

He leaned against the nearest shelf, arms crossed. "That book you keep coming back to. The black one. I saw it—once. A long time ago."

Layla's breath caught. "You've seen it?"

He nodded slowly, eyes suddenly clouded with memory. "It doesn't belong to this library. It doesn't belong to any catalog I've ever come across. Books, they usually age. Get brittle. This one... doesn't."

She stepped closer. "What do you know about it?"

Mr. Williams met her eyes. "Only this—it remembers. What you read, what you think. What you fear. And sometimes, it writes back."

Layla swallowed. "Why didn't you take it off the shelves?"

"Because I never put it there," he said quietly. "And when I tried to move it—it vanished. Until it decided to come back."

Her fingers curled slightly. The air felt heavier now, thick with unsaid things.

Mr. Williams's voice dropped lower. "Be careful, Miss Singh. Some stories don't just change lives. They rewrite them."

---

Layla sat alone at her usual corner table, the black book before her. Mr. Williams's warning rang in her ears, looping with every breath.

It remembers. It rewrites.

She stared at the book's worn cover, her hand hovering above it. For a moment, she didn't want to open it. But curiosity—dangerous, familiar—pulled her in again.

The pages were blank.

She flipped through them, faster and faster. Page after page of soft, yellowing emptiness.

And then, suddenly—ink.

Her fingers froze.

A new paragraph bloomed slowly across the center of the page, as though someone were writing it just then:

*"" She had been warned, but she opened the book anyway. Because some truths demand to be seen, even if they are the last thing you ever understand.""*

Layla's mouth went dry.

She slammed it shut, pushing it away like it had burned her fingertips. The silence around her thickened. Even the creak of the floorboards beneath her chair felt too loud.

She stood, heart thudding, and descended the stairs quickly. Mr. Williams glanced up but didn't say anything. He only watched her with eyes that seemed more tired than before.

Outside, the sun had begun to set, brushing the rooftops of Maplewood in strokes of soft amber and violet. Layla didn't realize how long she had stayed.

The evening air was cool against her cheeks, grounding. But as she walked home, her footsteps oddly mirrored the rhythm of the final sentence she read.

*" Even if they are the last thing you ever understand."*

She reached her house just as the streetlights blinked on. Her mom was in the kitchen, humming along to an old song on the radio. The scent of simmering curry greeted her like a warm blanket.

But even comfort now felt like an illusion.

Upstairs, in the quiet of her room, Layla reached under her bed and took out the book again.

This time, she didn't open it.

She just stared at it.

And it stared back.

# X

# Unseen Corners

Layla's alarm clock buzzed loudly, dragging her out of the depths of a restless sleep. She groggily reached out to silence it, her fingers brushing against the cool surface of her bedside table before landing on the familiar buttons. The room was still dark, the faint light of early morning creeping in through the blinds.

Sitting up slowly, Layla stretched and rubbed her eyes, letting the quiet of the morning wash over her for a moment. The usual hum of the world outside her window, the birds chirping, the distant sound of cars passing by, felt strangely absent.

She stood and walked to the bathroom, the cold tiles of the floor biting into her bare feet as she brushed her teeth. The mirror reflected a tired face, but it was her face, the same one she'd known for years. Yet something about the reflection seemed... distant. She couldn't place it. Maybe she was just still half asleep.

After a quick shower, Layla dressed in her usual outfit—a loose t-shirt, jeans, and sneakers. She didn't feel like picking anything special today. There was something about the dull routine that made it easier to slip into the motions, to pretend everything was normal.

Her mother was already in the kitchen, humming quietly as she flipped pancakes. The smell of syrup and warm batter filled the air, an aroma that usually made Layla feel comforted. But today, it felt distant—like a memory of something that used to make her happy.

"Morning, sweetie," her mother called, without turning around from the stove. Her voice had a strange flatness to it, like she was speaking from behind a wall.

"Morning, Mom," Layla replied, her voice slightly hesitant. She grabbed a piece of toast and sat down at the kitchen table, glancing at her phone. There were a few notifications from Ana, but she couldn't bring herself to read them just yet.

---

The streets were familiar—the cracked sidewalks near Cedar Street, the ivy-covered fence behind the post office, even the wind chime that always tinkled outside Mrs. Evans's antique shop. But today, they felt off. Less like home. More like a place built from memory... only not hers.

She passed the bakery on Main Street, where she and Ayaan used to split blueberry muffins. But the woman behind the counter didn't smile or wave like she usually did. In fact, she barely glanced up.

"Hi," Layla tried hesitantly, stepping closer. "I used to come here all the time."

The woman blinked, polite but distant. "I'm sorry, dear. I don't think I've seen you before."

Layla's heart thudded. She forced a laugh. "That's strange. I was here last week."

The woman gave a tight smile. "Maybe you're confusing it with somewhere else."

Layla backed out quietly, the door's bell sounding too loud behind her.

She wandered aimlessly, stopping at other places—her old art class above the florist, the bookshop that once carried second-hand poetry collections, the bus stop bench where she and Ana sat during late evening walks. But no one remembered her. No one even seemed to recognize her.

It was like she was... fading.

And then she saw Ryan.

He was leaning against the railing near Maplewood Park, earbuds in, scribbling something into his sketchbook. The sight of him—solid, real—was grounding. She almost ran to him.

"Hey," she called out.

He looked up instantly and smiled. "There you are."

She exhaled, a breath she hadn't realized she'd been holding. "Here I am."

"Everything okay? You look... like you saw a ghost."

Layla hesitated, then shook her head. "Just felt like walking. I needed a break from my thoughts."

"Same." He shut his sketchbook. "Want to sit?"

They walked together along the park path, side by side in the slow warmth of the day.

"I went to the bakery," she said quietly. "She didn't know me."

Ryan frowned. "Which one?"

"Mason's. We used to go there all the time, remember?"

"Of course." He gave a small nod. "That's weird. Maybe she forgot?"

"Maybe..." Her voice faltered. "Or maybe I'm forgetting who I am."

Ryan stopped walking and turned to face her. "Hey. You're Layla. The girl who always doodles in the corners of notebooks, drinks tea like it's a religion, and got me to read actual poetry. You're not disappearing."

She managed a weak smile. "You make it sound easy."

"I make it sound true."

They sat by the fountain where autumn leaves floated lazily across the surface. Layla didn't speak for a while, just let the silence wrap around them like a question waiting to be asked.

And somewhere deep in her bag, the book pulsed faintly.

The silence between them wasn't awkward. It was soft, full of unspoken things, as if both of them were trying to catch their breath from something they couldn't name.

Ryan leaned back on the bench, his fingers lightly drumming against his sketchbook. "You know, sometimes I think places hold memories. Like... echoes. The good kind. Maybe that's what you're feeling."

Layla glanced sideways at him. "And what if the echoes start leaving you behind?"

Ryan looked at her, his eyes steady. "Then we make new ones. Together."

Something in the way he said made her chest ache. It was safe. Simple. Human. And so starkly different from the way the world has been feeling lately.

She nodded and looked toward the water again. The leaves were turning gold, rust, and amber. Time was moving. But was she?

After a while, Ryan stood and stretched. "I should probably head back. Mom's making spaghetti and if I'm late, she'll say I've chosen starvation."

Layla laughed, genuinely. "You should go, then. Wouldn't want you wasting away."

He smiled down at her. "Hey... I'm around, okay? If anything feels off. Or if you just want to sit and talk about things that aren't creepy."

She stood too, brushing her hands on her jeans. "Thanks, Ryan. Really."

He hesitated, then stepped closer, brushing her knuckles with his. "You're not alone in this, Layla."And kissed gently on her cheek.

She watched him walk away, the space beside her suddenly too wide. As she turned back toward the path, a gust of wind fluttered the edges of her backpack. The book inside felt heavier now.

She walked slowly, tracing her way back toward The Lantern.

---

The library was empty. Unnaturally so. Not even the faint clicking of keyboards or the rustle of newspapers being turned. Just quiet—oppressive and still.

She stepped carefully down the rows, past familiar shelves. Her eyes landed on the fiction corner, where the armchair sat nestled under the tall window. It was there the book had first called her.

"Back again so soon?" a voice said, low and rough.

Layla turned sharply. Mr. Williams stood a few feet away, a cart of returned books in front of him. His gaze was unusually sharp.

"I didn't expect anyone today," he added.

"I needed... a place to think."

He nodded slowly. "That book. You still have it?"

Her fingers instinctively touched her bag. "Yes."

"I thought so." He wheeled the cart closer. "You should be careful with what you read in there."

Layla's skin crawled.

"Most people return it," he said. "Eventually. Or it finds its way back. But you..." He looked at her with something like pity. "It's still writing."

"What does it want?" Layla whispered.

Mr. Williams shook his head. "I don't think it knows. Not fully. But it clings. Especially to those who are already fading."

She staggered back a step. "Fading?"

"You should go home," he said quietly. "Before the next page turns."

---

That night, Layla sat cross-legged on her bed, the room dim except for the soft yellow glow of her lamp. Outside, the wind rattled the branches of the maple tree against her window, rhythmic and impatient.

The book rested on her blanket, closed but humming in its own silent way—like it was waiting.

Mr. Williams's words echoed in her mind:

"It clings. Especially to those who are already fading."

She wasn't fading. Was she?

Her fingers brushed over the cover. For a moment, she considered locking it away, shoving it into a drawer or hurling it out the window.

But something deeper tugged at her.

She flipped it open.

The pages fluttered on their own, stopping at a section that hadn't been there before. A blank page.

Her heart pounded.

And then, letter by letter, ink began to bloom across the white space—writing itself out in a slanted, spidery script.

Layla stared.

The words were forming her.

But they ended with something that made her blood run cold.

""*She will not be remembered.*""

# XI

# The Blank Page

Layla hadn't slept all night. Every time she closed her eyes, the words burned behind her eyelids—the ones she hadn't written, yet existed on the page."" She will not be remembered."" The sentence repeated in her mind like a whisper carried on wind, too quiet to catch, too loud to ignore.

By morning, the darkness under her eyes matched the shadows clouding her thoughts. She sat on the edge of her bed, staring at the book lying closed on her desk. It looked harmless now, but Layla knew better.

A sharp knock came at her door.

"Layla," her mother's voice called. "You'll be late for school."

Layla stood slowly. "I'm not feeling well," she said hoarsely.

The door opened slightly. Her mother peeked in, arms crossed. "You said that two days ago too. I don't want you falling behind."

"I really didn't sleep."

Her mom sighed. "You can nap in the afternoon. Just go. A walk in the fresh air might even help."

Layla hesitated, but finally nodded. She pulled on a hoodie, stuffed the book into her backpack like a weight she couldn't shake, and headed downstairs.

Her dad gave her a surprised glance over his coffee mug. "Morning."

"Morning," she mumbled.

"You look pale," he said. "Everything okay?"

Before she could respond, her mom chimed in from the kitchen. "She's fine. Just tired. Let's not make it worse with too much attention."

Layla left without breakfast. The sky was gray, the air still. Her mind was a fog of questions. What's happening to me?

She didn't go straight to school.

Instead, her feet carried her to the Lantern.

---

The Lantern was nearly empty when she arrived, its warm golden lights a soft contrast to the overcast morning. The scent of old pages and polished wood greeted her like a familiar friend—one of the few constants in a world that seemed to be shifting beneath her feet.

Mr. Williams looked up from the front desk, surprised. "You again? Shouldn't you be at school?"

"I needed... a quiet place."

He nodded slowly, watching her with a look that bordered on concern but didn't push further. "You know where everything is."

Layla went to her usual corner, the one beneath the slanted skylight where dust always danced in the sunlight. She took out the book and opened it cautiously, flipping to the pages she'd already read.

And then she saw it.

A new section had appeared. Previously, it had been blank—she was certain of it. But now the once-empty pages were filled with words written in the same thin, antique ink. She leaned closer, heart hammering.

*""She wandered farther from what tethered her to the world. Names began to vanish. Faces blurred. The lines thinned.""*

Layla swallowed hard.

She turned the page.

It was blank.

One single, ominous page—empty, waiting. She stared at it, a chill creeping along her spine. Something in her gut twisted. She reached into her backpack and pulled out a pen, tempted to test it—just one mark. Just a dot.

But her hand shook.

"You shouldn't try to change what's written," came Mr. Williams' voice from behind her. She flinched.

"I—I wasn't."

He looked at the book. His face, usually kind and composed, shifted into something unreadable. "That book is older than this library. It's meant to be read, not altered."

Layla's throat tightened. "What is it?"

He sat in the chair beside her, folding his hands. "It's a mirror, of sorts. And a trap. You read, and it writes you in. The more you look, the more it knows what to show."

"Why me?"

Mr. Williams gave a weary sigh. "Because you opened it. That's always how it starts."

Layla stared at the blank page again.

"What happens if I stop reading?" she whispered.

"I don't know," he said. "No one ever has."

---

The sky had darkened by the time Layla left The Lantern. A low mist curled around the streets of Maplewood, blurring the edges of houses and trees like smudges on a canvas. The book sat heavy in her backpack, as though it carried more than just paper and ink—something invisible, something watching.

She arrived at school halfway through the day. The halls were quieter than usual, the buzz of chatter and movement muted in her ears. A few students gave her puzzled glances as she made her way toward her locker, but no one said anything.

"Where were you?" Ryan's voice was gentle, but filled with concern as he caught up to her outside her next class.

"I just... needed some air," she said, avoiding his eyes.

Ryan frowned. "Layla, are you okay?"

She gave him a half-smile, the kind that didn't reach her eyes. "I will be."

They walked in silence for a moment until he reached out and gently brushed his fingers against hers. "You don't have to pretend with me, you know."

That warmth—the steady comfort of his presence—grounded her for a moment. "I know."

Lunch was quieter than usual too. Ana was off helping one of the photography teachers set up an exhibit, leaving Layla and Ryan alone at their usual table. Layla pushed the food around her tray, not feeling hungry. Ryan didn't press her with questions. Instead, he talked about practice, a funny moment in class, a new playlist he found. She let the sound of his voice steady her, let it distract her from the blank page that still lingered in her mind like a bruise.

When the final bell rang, they walked slowly toward the gate.

"Are you going to be okay?" Ryan asked.

"I think so," she replied. "I just need time."

He looked like he wanted to say more, but instead he pulled her close, pressing a kiss to the side of her head. "I'm here. Whenever you need."

As he jogged off toward the gym, Layla turned to head home.

But something in her felt altered.

Like the page—blank, waiting.

# XII

# Fractures

Layla paced by the window, tugging at the edge of her sleeve. The sky outside was dipped in grey, clouds hanging heavy like her thoughts. Her heart thudded faster than she liked to admit — not because of the cursed book tucked away in her drawer, but because Ryan was coming over. To her house. To meet her parents.

The Singh household sat quietly at the edge of Maplewood, a small two-story brick home with ivy creeping up the front and white-painted windows that always looked a little too clean. Her mother had a habit of wiping them twice a week — a small rebellion against the chaos of moving countries. Inside, the house smelled of sandalwood and fresh laundry, the hallway lined with framed photos from India: wedding pictures, Ayaan's first birthday, and one with Layla and Ana in front of the school library.

Layla's room was her sanctuary — tucked upstairs at the end of the hall, with pale green walls and shelves sagging under the weight of books. A dreamcatcher hung over her window, swaying slightly in the breeze, and a string of fairy lights outlined the headboard of her bed. Her desk was cluttered — notebooks, pens, and the ever-present book. The book.

She shoved it deep into her drawer and slammed it shut.

When the doorbell rang, her breath hitched. "Layla!" her mother called from downstairs. "He's here!"

Layla smoothed her hair, checked her reflection — and flinched. For a split second, it felt like her reflection had looked away before she did.

She pushed the thought aside and headed down.

Ryan stood at the door, his usual calm expression flickering with nerves. He held a small bouquet of daisies. "Hey," he said, and smiled.

Her parents were already in the living room — her father, sharp in a sweater vest, and her mother with her perpetual, assessing smile. "Come in, Ryan," her mother said, gracious but observant. "We've heard a lot about you."

Ryan offered the flowers, and Layla's mom accepted them with a nod. They sat down — the room suddenly too formal, as if time had slowed.

The conversation started awkwardly, hovering over school, Maplewood, and how long the Singhs had been in town. Her father asked about Ryan's family; her mother complimented his posture and the way he didn't slouch. Layla kept glancing at Ryan, hoping he didn't notice how tense she was.

But he was calm. He made them laugh. Even her father cracked a smile. And for a while, the shadows of the book, of the whispers, stayed tucked away.

But they didn't stay gone.

Ryan glanced around the hallway, eyes lingering on the little details that made the Singh household feel warm and lived-in — the polished wood floors, the faint scent of incense, the family photos that told a life before

Maplewood.

"Want to see my room?" Layla asked, voice soft, almost uncertain.

Ryan smiled gently. "Yeah. I'd like that."

She led him up the creaking staircase to the very last door on the left.

"Nice room," Ryan said as he stepped inside, taking it all in. The walls were pale sea green, and one side was covered in her sketches and small sticky notes with half-written thoughts. A single bookshelf near her desk held a mix of thriller and fantasy novels. A window overlooked the backyard, its curtains drawn halfway to let the sunset glow in.

Ryan sat on the bed, running his hand across the soft, worn blanket. "This feels... very you."

She sat beside him, and for a long moment, neither of them said anything. The silence wasn't awkward—it was charged, like they both were thinking the same thing.

"You've been... distracted lately," Ryan finally said. "Like something's always on your mind."

Layla hesitated. "I know. I'm sorry. I don't mean to push you away."

"I don't want to push," he said softly. "But I care. And I don't want to lose you to whatever it is that's pulling you under."

She looked at him—really looked. The way the dying sunlight caught the gold in his eyes. The concern in his voice. The care. And suddenly, something inside her ached to be close, to feel something real. Something she could hold on to.

Ryan cupped Layla's face with his calloused hands and leans in to kiss her. The kiss was slow, gentle. Not rushed. Like they were both trying to say a thousand things they didn't know how to speak aloud.

Her hands found his, fingers lacing together. He pulled her closer, their foreheads touching. He tucked her hair behind her ear so that he could kiss her with even more passion.

"I'm right here," he whispered. "Whatever this is, we'll face it. Together."

But as his words echoed, her eyes flicked toward the desk—where the book lay waiting.

---

After Ryan left, Layla stood at her window for a long time, watching his silhouette grow smaller under the amber streetlights until it disappeared around the corner. Her heart was still fluttering, her lips tingling from the warmth of his kiss. Yet beneath that blooming emotion, something colder curled.

The book.

It hadn't moved from the drawer, yet it felt alive.

She opened it with trembling fingers. The pages greeted her like an old friend she no longer trusted. And then she saw it—the blank section. Still eerily pristine, like it had been waiting for her.

She sat at her desk, the lamp casting long shadows on the wall. After a moment of hesitation, she reached for a pen.

"What if I could control what happens next?" she wrote. Her hand shook. "What if I could change the story before it changes me?"

The ink bled slightly into the old paper. For a second, nothing happened.

Then the words vanished.

The page turned by itself.

New lines began to form—written in the same sharp, jagged script she'd seen before:

*""The moment you believe you're the author, the book reminds you—you are still a character.""*

Goosebumps prickled her arms. The room seemed darker. The lamp flickered once.

And then, beneath that line, one final sentence appeared:

*""You shouldn't have let him in.""*

# XIII
## Voices Of The Ink

The chill in the air was gentler that morning, yet Layla felt unsettled as she stepped outside. The sky wore a pale, washed-out blue, and a faint breeze tugged at her sweater sleeves. Ana had texted her early—"Let's hang out? Starbucks?"—and Layla didn't hesitate. She needed the noise, the normalcy, the distraction.

Starbucks was alive with chatter and the hum of espresso machines. The scent of roasted coffee beans and cinnamon swirled around them as they found a corner booth by the window. Sunlight streamed through the glass, turning Ana's hair almost bronze.

"I'm glad you're out," Ana said, stirring her frappuccino. "You've seemed... distracted lately."

Layla smiled faintly. "Yeah. Just school and stuff."

Ana tilted her head. "And Ryan?"

A small warmth fluttered in Layla's chest. "He's been... really sweet. I think I'm lucky."

Ana changes the topic and says, "I swear," she grinned, checking the photo, "if you ever become a ghost, I'll still photograph you."

Layla smiled. "Wouldn't the photos be blank then?"

Ana winked. "Even then. I'd caption them: 'Spotted: Layla's ghost ordering a latte.'"

They both laughed. For a moment, the tension eased.

The scent of cinnamon and steamed milk wrapped around her like a hug. It should have been comforting.

But beneath the music, beneath the low murmur of voices, something else stirred. A sound only Layla heard.

Whispers.

They weren't faint anymore. They were distinct—syllables curling like smoke, rising from the book even though it remained closed in her bag.

She tried to ignore it. Ana was holding up her phone, framing a selfie of the two of them.

"Smile, Layla!"

Layla leaned in. Forced a grin. Click.

Another photo. Then a boomerang of them clinking mugs. Ana giggled and typed up a caption for her story: "Book besties and caffeine queens."

Layla reached for her phone to see it. In the boomerang, her mug clinked against Ana's—but her own face was strangely blurred, like a smudge on the lens.

"Ana... can I see that again?"

Ana tilted the screen toward her. "Yeah? Something wrong?"

Layla stared. The blur was subtle—but it was there. Her outline looked less real than Ana's. As if she was already fading.

But then the whispers returned.

Muffled at first, like someone talking from behind a wall. Then sharper. Clearer.

*"Blood on the road. Screams in the dark."*

Layla stiffened. She glanced around. No one else noticed. Ana was still typing away on her phone.

"Stop," Layla whispered under her breath, clutching her bag tighter. The book. It was with her. She hadn't opened it today. Hadn't even thought about it—

*"He won't come back the same," the voice hissed again."*

She stood abruptly.

Ana looked up. "Layla? You okay?"

"I—I have to go. I'm sorry."

"Wait, what happened?"

But Layla was already rushing out the door, the whisper repeating in her mind like a warning bell.

---

The streets blurred past as Layla sprinted, her heart pounding. The sun had dipped lower now, and shadows stretched long over the pavement. She headed toward the basketball courts. She was not breathing as she reached the ground. Maybe he was still there—maybe—

Screams.

A screech of tires.

People gathering.

Her lungs nearly gave out as she reached the scene. An ambulance. A broken bike twisted on the curb. And Ryan—

Ryan on the ground.

His body was still. Blood pooled from a wound on his head. A paramedic was pressing gauze to his side, shouting something Layla couldn't hear through the ringing in her ears.

"No..." she choked, pushing past someone. "That's—Ryan—please let me—"

A firm arm held her back. "You can't be here, miss."

"But I—he's—"

Ryan's eyes fluttered briefly, and he turned his head slightly. His gaze found her. A pained, confused flicker of recognition.

"Layla..." he murmured. And then he slipped into unconsciousness.

Tears streamed down her face. The book's voice echoed again:

*""It's only the beginning.""*

# XIV

## The Forgotten Photo

Layla couldn't sleep the whole night. She begged her parents to let her go to the hospital at night so she could be with Ryan. She wanted to feel him ; She wanted him to be okay. But her parents refused and asked her to meet him at the hospital Tomorrow morning.

All night Layla sobbed into her pillow, thinking about how because of her, her friends , family , and even ryan now is in danger.

She stood outside the hospital room, lavender flowers in her hand, feeling a tightness in her chest that wouldn't ease no matter how many deep breaths she took. She had come straight from school, trying to ignore the unease that had been gnawing at her all day. Ryan had been in the hospital, and the guilt that weighed on her had only grown heavier with each passing hour. She wasn't sure how she was supposed to feel anymore, but she knew she couldn't stand the thought of him alone in there, suffering.

She stepped inside, her heart pounding as she caught sight of him. Ryan was lying in the bed, an array of bandages wrapping his arm and leg, his forehead marked by a small cut that had been stitched up. The room smelled of antiseptic, but all Layla could focus on was him. She felt a wave of emotion rising—he looked so fragile, so unlike the boy who had been full of life just a few days ago. Her stomach churned with the realization of how close she had come to losing him.

He looked up when she entered, his lips curving into a tired but genuine smile. "Hey," he greeted softly, his voice hoarse.

"Hi," Layla whispered, her voice cracking as she stepped toward him, placing the lavender flowers carefully on the bedside table. She stood for a moment, watching him, before she finally sat down on the chair beside his bed. Her fingers lightly brushed against his, but the silence between them was thick and heavy.

"I'm sorry," she blurted out suddenly, her voice shaky. "This is all my fault. If I hadn't—"

"Layla," Ryan interrupted gently, his free hand reaching for hers, his grip warm and firm. "You didn't do this. It wasn't your fault."

But she couldn't shake the feeling that it was her fault. She had been so consumed by the strange pull of the book and the whispers that seemed to control everything around her, and now Ryan was paying the price. She squeezed her eyes shut, trying to hold back the tears, but it was no use. The floodgates opened, and she burst into tears, her body shaking with the force of her emotions.

"I'm so scared, Ryan," she sobbed, her face buried in her hands. "I don't know what's happening, I don't know what to do. I keep hearing these whispers, and I—"

Ryan's voice was soothing, even though he was still so weak. "Hey, it's okay. I'm here. We'll figure this out together. You're not alone in this."

Layla looked up at him, her eyes filled with unshed tears. His warm smile never wavered, even as he struggled to sit up a little more in the bed. Slowly, he opened his arms, and Layla didn't hesitate to move closer. She leaned into him, her head resting on his chest as he wrapped his arms around her. The warmth of his embrace was like a lifeline, a comforting reassurance that he was still here, still alive.

"I don't want to lose you," Layla whispered, her voice muffled against his shirt. "I can't."

Ryan tightened his hold on her, his voice a soft murmur. "You won't. I'm not going anywhere, Layla. I promise."

The tears kept coming, but this time they weren't just from fear. They were from a place of relief, of love, of knowing that she wasn't alone anymore. He was here with her, and for the first time in days, Layla allowed herself to feel the hope that had been buried beneath all the fear.

The door to the room creaked open, and Layla's head lifted as she saw Ana walk in, holding a large bouquet of tulips. Ana's eyes immediately softened when she saw the two of them together, and she smiled faintly, though the concern in her gaze was impossible to miss.

"I brought tulips," Ana said, her voice light, but her eyes flickered to Ryan with a quiet understanding. "And I... I also brought this." She reached into her bag and pulled out a framed photo—a picture of the three of them together, from the day they had spent at the park, laughing and carefree. Ana handed it to Layla, who took it with trembling hands.

For a moment, everything seemed normal. The photo showed the three of them—Layla, Ana, and Ryan—smiling brightly, the sun shining in the background, carefree. It was a memory of better times. Layla smiled through her tears, a small chuckle escaping her lips as she looked at the happy image.

But then, something strange happened. She felt a slight chill run down her spine as she stared at the photo, her gaze lingering on the familiar faces. Something wasn't right.

"Ana," Layla said, her voice barely a whisper, "can you see it?"

Ana frowned and leaned in closer, looking at the picture. "See what?"

Layla pointed. "Right here. I'm—I'm fading."

Ana's smile faltered as she looked closer. Her face paled. "Wait... what the hell?"

Ryan tried to sit up, groaning from the effort. "What is it?"

Layla stared at the photo, horror crawling up her spine like ice. She wasn't just fading.

She was almost completely gone.

# XV

## Cracks In The Reality

A week had passed since Ryan's accident. The stitches near his brow were healing well, the bruises on his ribs were no longer a deep violet, and his voice had regained its usual warmth, though his smiles came slower. Layla had visited the hospital every day, lavender flowers in her hands, guilt in her heart. And now, he was back home, safe. Or so it seemed.

But the world around Layla was no longer the same.

It began with small things—an absence of acknowledgment, a strange tilt of the head, a pause too long when someone looked at her.

She stood at her locker in the hallway of Riverstone High, her fingers tracing the familiar edge of her mirror sticker, the one Ana had gifted her on the first day of junior year. But as she turned to wave at her chemistry teacher, Mrs. Holt, who always greeted her with a smile, the woman walked right past her, as if Layla were the breeze brushing by—not a student who had once aced her pop quiz, who had once spilled an entire beaker and laughed until Mrs. Holt cracked a rare grin.

The first sting.

Then came the second.

In the homeroom, Mr. Beale paused when calling roll. "Andrew Johnson?"

"Here," Andrew said, raising his hand.

"Ana Lopez?"

"Here."

The teacher frowned slightly at the clipboard. "Hmm... I must've made a mistake."

He never said Layla's name.

She blinked, confused. "Mr. Beale?" she called, quietly.

He didn't even look up. No one did.

Ana sat just a few feet away, flipping through her camera roll on her phone. Layla leaned closer and whispered, "Hey, did he just skip me?"

Ana didn't respond at first. "Huh?"

"I'm not on the attendance sheet," Layla said. "You noticed, right?"

Ana stared at her for a moment, her brow furrowed. "I... I think so. I don't know, maybe he's just tired."

Layla's heart dropped. Ana hesitated. Ana never hesitates.

Later that afternoon, Ryan met her near the library steps. The bruises had faded, and he looked more like himself again—messy hair, hoodie sleeves too long over his hands. His smile widened as he saw her. For a second, all felt right.

"I'm starving," he said. "Can we grab a sandwich before rehearsal?"

Layla smiled weakly. "Sure. Ryan... Can I ask you something weird?"

"Only if I get a bite of your sandwich," he teased.

"Do you remember when we met?"

Ryan chuckled. "Yeah. You were the quiet girl who wouldn't talk to anyone and read during lunch. You were walking the aisle down the lantern when I approached you."

Layla smiled at the memory. "Right. And... do you remember our first date?"

He paused. "Of course. We went to—" He stopped, brows furrowed. "Wait. Was it the bookstore café or the diner?"

"Bookstore café," she said quietly.

He laughed it off. "Sorry, my brain's still fuzzy from the concussion. It'll come back."

But that night, Layla cried herself to sleep.

---

The next morning, she marched to the front office of the school. The lady behind the desk wore thick glasses and a Riverstone alumni sweatshirt.

"Hi, I was wondering if I could get a copy of my school record? Or just confirm something in the system?"

The woman smiled. "Name?"

"Layla Singh. Grade 11."

Clicking. Typing. Pause.

"Sorry, could you spell that?"

Layla did.

Another pause.

"I don't have Layla Singh on file."

Her stomach dropped. "That's impossible. I've been here since junior year."

The woman frowned, turned the screen slightly. "There's no Singh family listed in our student database. Are you sure you're not a transfer who hasn't been updated yet?"

"I— No, this is a mistake."

"You can talk to the counselor. She handles records."

Layla left without speaking another word. Her hands were shaking.

She wasn't just being forgotten—she was being erased.

---

That afternoon, she knocked on Ana's door, tears already forming in her eyes. Ana opened it, surprised, her camera hanging around her neck.

"Layla?"

"I need to talk to you."

Ana nodded and stepped aside, letting her in.

They sat on Ana's bed, cross-legged. Layla pulled out her journal—the one she'd been keeping since the book first began changing her world.

"Things are getting worse," she whispered. "Ryan forgot our first date. The school doesn't have me on record. Even Mrs. Holt walked right past me."

Ana's expression darkened. "That doesn't make sense. I remember you being here. Ryan does too."

Layla looked up. "Do you really? Do you remember our first day of school?"

Ana hesitated. "Of course."

"What was I wearing?"

"Um... jeans?"

"You took a picture of us that day."

Ana pulled out her phone, flipping back. When she found the photo and held it up, Layla gasped.

It was a photo of Ana in front of Riverstone High, throwing a peace sign. But Layla wasn't beside her.

"I was standing right next to you," she whispered.

Ana's lips parted in confusion. "I... I swear you were."

"I'm being erased, Ana."

---

Layla walked home alone, her hoodie pulled tight around her face, the chill in the air echoing the frost now forming around her soul. The leaves crackled beneath her shoes, and every sound—distant laughter, the chirp of a bird, the hum of passing cars—seemed to exist in a world she no longer belonged to.

She barely registered the creak of the gate as she entered her front yard.

Her house stood quietly under the shade of the eucalyptus trees, two stories of comfort and warm memories, painted pale cream with maroon shutters. A pot of marigolds sat by the porch steps—her mother's touch—and the wind chimes jingled softly above the front door. From the outside, everything looked the same.

Inside, it felt foreign.

She entered and shut the door gently behind her. The usual scent of cardamom and cinnamon still lingered from the evening chai, but instead of soothing her, it clawed at her nerves. She passed the living room, where Ayaan had left his LEGOs scattered like little landmines, and climbed the stairs, each one groaning under her weight like it could sense the dread she carried.

Her room welcomed her with familiarity: the galaxy fairy lights across the ceiling, her soft beige and navy comforter, the paper cranes taped above her mirror, and the framed polaroid of her, Ana, and Ryan on the shelf. The one Ana hadn't taken—but one Layla remembered capturing herself.

She stared at the photo now. She wasn't in it anymore.

Tears welled up again. She dropped onto her bed, curling into a ball, her head sinking into the pillow. Her chest ached, not just with sadness, but with something deeper—like her very existence was unraveling thread by thread.

Why me?

Why this book?

She hadn't touched it in days. After the accident, she'd shoved it into the drawer under her desk, vowing not to read another word. But the silence hadn't helped. The questions were louder than the whispers now.

She sat up slowly, her body moving on instinct, and reached into the drawer.

The book was still there—black leather, cold to the touch despite the warmth of her room. The gold-etched title shimmered unnaturally in the dim light, like it was waiting.

She brought it to her desk and lit the candle Ana had gifted her last Christmas. The soft lavender scent mixed with the storm brewing in her heart.

The book fell open to the exact place she'd left it.

Only now, more words have appeared.

> "*"You cannot outrun a story already written, Layla. You can only read it to its end."*"

She slammed it shut, her heart pounding. "I'm not a story," she whispered. "I'm real."

But the doubt was there.

Real people don't fade from photographs.

Real people don't vanish from memory.

She pressed her forehead to the book, trembling.

What if I was never real to begin with?

Her tears fell silently, sinking into the pages.

# XVI

## Echoes Of Her Name

The knock came just after nine. Ana had barely touched her cereal when she heard it, sharp and hurried. When she opened the door, Ryan stood on her porch, his hair a little messy, dark circles under his eyes like he hadn't slept. In his hand was a notebook, corners bent, pages bulging with added scraps of paper.

"I think we need to talk," he said quietly.

Ana stepped aside. "Come in."

Her house smelled of brewed coffee and lemon cleaner. A glass of orange juice sat half-drunk on the coffee table. The curtains were half-drawn, letting in a haze of morning light that settled over the living room like dust. Ryan sat stiffly on the edge of the sofa while Ana perched on the armrest across from him, hugging a throw pillow against her chest.

"Something's wrong," Ryan began. He ran a hand through his hair. "With Layla. With me. I keep forgetting things. I looked through my texts with her and... some are missing. Others don't make sense. And yesterday, I was staring at a class photo and couldn't find her in it. Not even in the background."

Ana nodded slowly. "It's not just you. I've been thinking the same.

"We have to find the truth. ryan paused . About the book and layla"

The soft hum of Ana's laptop filled the quiet room, broken only by the occasional clack of keys and Ryan's sighs as he scrolled through pages on his phone. Ana sat cross-legged on her bed, her hoodie sleeves pushed up, hair messily tied, a steaming mug of coffee untouched on the desk nearby. The sun had set hours ago, and the glow of the screen made the shadows on the walls feel deeper, heavier.

"I've searched for every Layla Singh in Maplewood's records and school archives," Ryan muttered, brows furrowed. "None match our Layla."

"Same," Ana whispered, her eyes not leaving the screen. "But I'm not giving up. We'll find something. There has to be something."

They had started with public records, school websites, and archived newsletters. Riverstone High's site had no mention of Layla on any student list or club photo. No yearbook pictures. No mentions of awards. Not even a digital footprint. It was like she had never attended the school.

"She's been in your class, right?" Ryan asked suddenly. "You remember her sitting next to you?"

Ana nodded slowly. "Yeah, I do. I mean... I think I do."

Ryan stared at her. "Think?"

"It's just—some memories feel... fuzzy. Like when you try to remember a dream after waking up." She tapped his temple. "The emotion is there, but the details feel off."

Ana turned her laptop screen toward him. "Explain this. I found the 2023 Riverstone yearbook online. Check the sophomore class photos."

They zoomed in.

Ryan blinked. "She's not there?"

"No. Even in the group shots. Nothing." Ana's voice trembled. "But look—there's space. Like... people are standing as if someone should be there."

Ryan leaned closer. In one photo, a hand rested on someone's shoulder—except no one was in that spot. Another showed a girl mid-laugh, eyes clearly aimed at someone beside her, but the space was empty.

Ana switched tabs. "I cross-referenced the Maplewood Gazette's obituaries from the past ten years. At first, nothing. But then I searched not for 'Layla Singh'... but for 'unidentified teenage girl' and narrowed it by date and location."

Her voice quieted. "Look at this."

On the screen was a scanned article from nearly two years ago. "Mysterious Death in Maplewood Library: Girl Found Dead, Identity Unknown." The image was grainy, taken outside The Lantern. Police tape. A stretcher. A girl's pale arm dangling, fingers curled slightly.

"No ID. No family came forward. They buried her as Jane Doe," Ana whispered. "The article says she was found with... a book in her lap."

Ryan's throat went dry.

"A black book," Ana continued. "With no title."

They sat in silence, staring.

"This is her," Ryan finally said. "This is Layla."

"But how?" Ana's voice broke. "She's alive. She's with us."

"Or the book..." Ryan stood abruptly, pacing. "The book re-wrote her. Gave her a new story. A new life. Inserted her into our world."

Ana slowly nodded. "Which is why she's vanishing. She wasn't meant to exist anymore. The rewrite is unraveling."

They looked at each other, the weight of it crashing down.

"We need answers. Real ones. From the source."Ryan exclaimed

Ana looked up, already knowing who he meant.

"Mr. Williams," they said together.

---

The air was sharp with the crispness of maple leaves crunching beneath their shoes as Ana and Ryan walked side by side down Maple Street. The streets were quiet, lined with amber trees and the occasional sound of a car passing by. The Lantern stood in the distance, dark and looming, waiting.

Neither of them spoke for a while. Ana shoved her hands into her pockets, her fingers curled tightly into fists. Ryan kept his eyes down, watching the pavement shift under their steps.

"She's not just a girl we care about," Ana finally said, her voice low. "She's... someone whose existence shouldn't even be real. Do you realize how terrifying that is?"

Ryan nodded. "Yeah. It's like we've been living inside a lie without knowing it. I keep trying to trace back all our memories—when I first spoke to her, when we became close—but now it all feels... brittle. Like glass ready to crack."

Ana stopped walking for a second. "But she's still real to us. She laughs. She gets angry. She cries. She reads and worries and dreams. Even if the book created her—"

"She's not just words on a page," Ryan finished softly.

Ana's eyes brimmed with tears, but she blinked them back. "Exactly."

They walked again, slower now.

"I keep thinking about the group photo," she whispered. "How she just... disappeared from it. Like a ghost being erased. I've never felt anything like that. It makes me question what memory even is."

Ryan looked at her. "What scares me the most is that... I might forget her too. I already feel parts of her slipping. I tried remembering the exact color of her favorite sweater yesterday. I couldn't. But I remember how she smiled when she wore it."

"That's the thing, Ryan." Ana's voice cracked. "Even if we lose her... I don't want to lose the feeling of her."

Ryan stopped walking. "I think I love her."

Ana stared at him.

"I didn't know it until now. Or maybe I did and I was scared to admit it. But everything we're finding—every impossible thing—is making it clearer. I'd go back in time or rewrite every chapter if it meant saving her."

Ana placed a hand on his arm. "Then we fight. With whatever we've got. If there's a way to pull her out of the book's grip, we'll find it."

They continued down the sidewalk, the Lantern looming closer with every step.

"She deserves to know the truth," Ana said. "No more secrets."

"But how do you tell someone that they died once? That they're living a borrowed story?" Ryan asked.

"With compassion," Ana said. "And with hope."

The Lantern's shadow finally touched their feet as they stopped outside its old wooden door. Ryan stared at the familiar sign above it, his hand reaching for the handle.

Ana took a deep breath. "Let's find out who wrote the first draft of her story."

Ryan nodded, heart pounding. "Let's find Mr. Williams."

# XVII
## Confessions

The sky above Maplewood was painted in shades of gray, heavy clouds sagging under the weight of the coming storm. Ana and Ryan walked side by side toward The Lantern Library, the silence between them dense with everything unsaid. The discovery they had made haunted them—the name, the face, the yearbook. It wasn't someone like Layla. It was Layla.

Ryan kept pulling out his phone, as if double-checking would make the image disappear. But there she was again—Layla Singh, 15 years ago. The same delicate features, that quiet smile. It didn't make sense, and yet it explained too much.

As they stepped into the library, the familiar creak of the wooden floor beneath them felt foreign now, eerie in its quiet echo. The scent of old books and varnished oak hit them like a memory. Dust floated in lazy spirals in the shafts of gray light filtering through the windows.

Mr. Williams sat at the front desk, his reading glasses low on his nose, absorbed in an ancient tome. He looked up as the door opened and froze.

"Ana. Ryan." His voice was a quiet tremor. "Didn't expect you two to be here together."

Ana stepped forward, her voice steady but strained. "We need to talk. It's about Layla."

Mr. Williams' hand paused mid-page. "Layla?"

"We found her," Ryan said. "Or who she used to be. There was a death notice. A yearbook. A photograph."

"She's our best friend," Ana added. "And we deserve the truth."

The old man's gaze dropped to his hands. His mouth pressed into a thin line. Then, slowly, he rose. "Follow me."

He led them past towering shelves and whispered memories, into the back hallway marked STAFF ONLY. He pulled a ring of iron keys from his pocket and opened the old door at the end.

A cold breeze met them as they descended the narrow spiral staircase. The air grew damp. At the bottom: a heavy wooden door. Mr. Williams unlocked it.

Inside was a room frozen in time. Filing cabinets lined the walls, and in the center sat a long oak table. On it lay a single book—weathered, frayed at the edges, it's cover a dull, leathery black. No title. Just age and silence.

Mr. Williams walked to it with reverence. "This," he said softly, "is the book Layla found."

He looked at Ana and Ryan, pain flickering behind his glasses. "You deserve to know everything."

He exhaled a long breath. "Layla Singh was the first reader. Fifteen years ago. She was a quiet girl. She came here almost every afternoon after school. Obsessed with stories. One day, she wandered too far into the archives and found this."

He touched the book like it might vanish. "She took it home. I should've stopped her. She read it cover to cover in a week."

"What happened?" Ryan asked.

Mr. Williams' eyes clouded. "She vanished. They found her body in the woods—cold, drenched, still holding the book. But when we opened it... the blank pages had changed. The story was about her. Her name. Her thoughts. Her death. Her rebirth."

Ana's breath hitched. "You mean—?"

He nodded. "The book wrote her back. But not as she was. It wrote her differently. Wove her into a new story. She returned... but not alive, not in the way we understand it. More like a... character."

Ryan recoiled slightly. "And we—everyone—we just accepted it?"

"The book makes people forget," Mr. Williams said bitterly. "It changes things—memories, files, records. Makes her story real for everyone else. But some of us—those tied to the library, to the book—we remember."

He reached into a drawer and pulled out a folder. Inside was a single photograph. A teenage girl stood in front of the library gates. Same long hair. Same eyes. Same Layla.

"This was taken two weeks before she died," Mr. Williams whispered. "We tried to destroy the book. Fire. Water. Even burial. But it comes back. And each time... the story resets."

Ryan stared at the photo, disbelief turning into horror. "How many times has this happened?"

"I don't know," Mr. Williams said. "I only remember her story. But I believe there have been others."

Ana's hands trembled. "So when she finishes reading it—?"

Mr. Williams nodded gravely. "Her story ends. She fades again. And the book begins again."

The old bulb overhead flickered.

Ana clutched the photo. "We have to tell her."

"She won't believe you," Mr. Williams said. "Not until the very end. When the truth becomes too loud to silence."

Ryan's voice was barely a whisper. "Is there any way to save her?"

A long pause.

Mr. Williams shook his head. "You can try. But stories don't like being rewritten."

As they walked back upstairs, Ana's phone buzzed.

*Hey! Feeling better. Want to hang tomorrow? Miss you guys.*

She stared at the message, tears lining her eyes.

Ryan leaned over. "She has no idea."

Ana's fingers hovered over the keyboard. Then she typed: *"Sure. Tomorrow."*

Outside, the storm cracked open, the sky weeping for a truth too heavy to bear

# XVIII
## Denial

The sky was bruised with the colors of dusk as Layla stepped away from Ana's house, her footsteps uncertain on the damp pavement. The air was heavy, humming with a tension she couldn't name. Ana's strange demeanor, her forced smile, the way she looked at Layla like she was trying to memorize her—all of it haunted her.

She pulled her hoodie tighter around her and took the long way home, hoping the walk would clear the fog that had settled in her chest. Her thoughts churned like the clouds above, unsettled and dark.

When she finally reached home, her house stood quiet and warm, golden light spilling from the kitchen windows. Inside, the comfort of familiarity wrapped around her like a blanket. The scent of masala drifted through the air, and she heard Ayaan's laughter from the living room.

"Layla?" her mother called from the kitchen. "You're just in time for dinner."

She managed a small smile and kicked off her shoes. "Smells good."

They sat down together at the table—her parents, Ayaan, and her. The clink of utensils and casual conversation filled the room. Her father teased Ayaan about his obsession with dinosaurs. Her mother reminded them about a family movie night on Saturday. Everything was normal.

Except it wasn't.

Layla felt like a ghost among them. Her hands moved on autopilot, bringing food to her mouth, but her thoughts were far away. The book. The whispers. The strange way the lines changed when she wasn't looking.

After dinner, she helped clean up, hugged Ayaan goodnight, and retreated to her room.

The book waited for her on her desk.

She stared at it for a long time, then slowly sat down and flipped it open. The pages fluttered, almost like they were breathing. New text had appeared:

*""The girl walks unknowingly toward her truth, unaware of the grave that already bears her name.""*

Her stomach turned.

She flipped ahead—pages that had been blank now filled with details. Conversations she hadn't had yet. Places she hadn't gone. But one line chilled her the most:

*""When the mirror cracks, so does her name.""*

She slammed the book shut and shoved it away. Her breathing was shallow, and her hands trembled. Every instinct screamed at her to run, to pretend none of it was real. But deep down, she knew she couldn't hide from this anymore.

Hours passed. She lay in bed, staring at the ceiling as rain began to tap lightly against the windows. Her parents had gone to bed, the house now draped in silence.

She sat up.

With quiet, practiced movements, she slipped on her shoes, grabbed a flashlight, and tucked the book into her backpack. Her phone buzzed with a text from Ana, but she didn't check it.

The front door creaked as she opened it, and a gust of cool air rushed in. She stepped out into the night.

Maplewood was asleep. Streetlights flickered, puddles reflected the storm-churned sky, and the wind whispered through the trees. She walked quickly, her heart pounding louder than her footsteps.

The Lantern Library loomed ahead, its windows dark. She circled around to the back, where a small side window was cracked open just enough. She hesitated only a moment before pushing it wider and climbing through.

Inside, the library was a cathedral of silence. Every creak of the wooden floor echoed. Guided by the weak beam of her flashlight, she made her way past shelves, past the reading alcove, to the hallway that led to the archive room.

The door was locked.

But Layla remembered how Mr. Williams had used a bobby pin to open an old cabinet once. She dug into her backpack, found a hairpin, and fumbled with the lock until it clicked open.

The air inside was cold and dry. Filing cabinets lined the walls, their drawers labeled with yellowing stickers.

She pulled open the drawer marked "Obituaries." Her fingers skimmed through paper after paper. Nothing.

Then she saw it.

"Singh, Layla."

Her hand froze. She pulled the folder out with shaking hands and opened it.

A photograph fell out.

Her face stared back at her—slightly younger, her hair shorter, but it was undeniably her. The name beneath it: Layla Singh (1995-2010)

Cause of death: Accidental drowning.

Location: Maplewood Cemetery.

Her breath hitched. She clutched the photo to her chest, her heart hammering.

"No," she whispered.

She turned and ran.

The rain was coming down harder now, soaking her within seconds. Thunder cracked overhead as she sprinted down the road, muddy water splashing around her feet.

The cemetery gates groaned as she pushed them open. Lightning illuminated rows of headstones like ghostly soldiers.

She searched frantically, heart screaming in her chest.

Then she saw it.

A small, moss-covered gravestone near a willow tree. The inscription barely visible in the rain:

LAYLA SINGH

Beloved Daughter

1995-2010

She collapsed to her knees.

"This isn't real," she whispered, hands trembling as they reached out to touch the cold stone. "This isn't me."

But it was.

Tears mingled with the rain as she cried, her sobs lost to the wind. She clutched the book to her chest, wanting to tear it apart, to scream until the grave vanished.

Lightning split the sky again.

She pressed her forehead to the gravestone, broken. The rain kept falling, drowning everything in its path, even the sound of her pain.

In the distance, a bell tolled once.

And the book pulsed in her hands.

# XIX

## Letting Go

The sky was quiet the next morning. Almost too quiet. Not the calm that follows a storm, but the hush that comes when the world knows something is about to end.

Layla sat on the windowsill of her bedroom, knees tucked beneath her chin, watching the golden light pour over Maplewood like a last goodbye. The town stirred gently—cars hummed by, a dog barked, wind rustled through trees—but inside her, everything was still. Numb. Hollow.

Her eyes drifted to the book resting on her desk. Its cover, once mysterious and intriguing, now looked like a trap—one she had walked into with wide eyes and an open heart. It waited, patient and silent, the way predators do.

She hadn't opened it since the night before.

Since she'd seen her own name carved into cold stone.

Since the thunder had cried with her.

She curled tighter into herself, memories flickering like fading Polaroids in her mind: Ana's laughter, Ryan's quiet gaze, Ayaan's jokes, her mother's cooking, her father's stories.

Were they ever real?

Or had they been ink?

---

By evening, the shadows grew longer, stretching like claws across her room. The book remained unopened, but she could feel it now—whispering in the corner of her mind. Calling.

She wandered the house one more time like a ghost previewing her own absence. The scent of masala and coriander still lingered in the kitchen, remnants of dinner she hadn't touched. Her mother was on the couch, one arm curled around a cushion, glasses slipping down her nose. Her father sat beside her, snoring softly, the TV casting flickering blue shadows across their resting faces.

Ayaan's door was shut, faint music drifting out. She hesitated outside it, hand hovering over the handle.

He had been the first real tether she felt after returning. Always nosy, always loud, but always there.

She wanted to knock. To say something. Anything.

Instead, she whispered through the wood: "Goodbye."

Then, without waiting for a response, she returned to her room.

The book was waiting.

She sat at her desk, heart pounding so loudly it drowned out every whisper the book tried to make. With trembling fingers, she opened it.

The pages were near the end now. Only a few left.

She skimmed the sentences. They described things exactly as they were: the creak of her chair, the pulse in her wrist, the tears that hadn't even fallen yet.

Each word felt heavier than the last. Each sentence, a stitch coming undone in the fabric of her reality.

She turned the page.

And there it was.

The final chapter.

It was titled **"Letting Go."**

Her breath caught.

The words described her room exactly as it was. The smell of lavender, the faded posters, the chipped blue paint on her bookshelf. It described her sitting on the bed, the book in her lap. It described her heartbeat. Her tears. Her thoughts.

She tried to stop.

Tried to close the book.

But her hands moved on their own.

She kept reading.

Her eyes devoured every word, even as her vision blurred. The story told of her death—not violent, not loud. Just fading. Like morning mist under sunlight. Her skin becoming light. Her voice becoming silence.

The words described her memories unspooling, threads being pulled gently away—first the sound of Ana's voice, then Ryan's laugh, then Ayaan's hug, then her own reflection.

She reached the second-last page.

By now, her hands looked pale. Almost translucent. She could see the faint shadow of the blanket through her fingers.

Her breath hitched.

She wasn't ready.

But maybe she never would be.

---

She stood up, the book still in hand, and walked to the mirror.

No reflection.

Just the room.

She reached out and touched the glass. It was cold.

A sob built in her throat, but it didn't come out.

Instead, she remembered:

Ana's arms around her after a bad day.

Ryan's voice as he told her she mattered.

Ayaan standing up for her at school, silly and brave.

Her mother's curry on rainy days. Her father's old, groan-worthy jokes.

None of it had been fake.

Not to her.

And if it felt real—if it had brought her joy and pain and warmth—then maybe it would've been real enough.

Behind her, the book's final page fluttered in the breeze from the open window.

She turned.

The last line was waiting.

*""And so she let go.""*

She read it aloud, her voice thin and shaky.

And something inside her gave way.

---

She didn't feel pain.

Only lightness.

Her body dissolved into dust and whispers, into the scent of forgotten pages and the hum of stories that remember.

The book closed itself gently.

The room was still.

Silent.

But if someone had walked in, they might have noticed the lavender scent lingering in the air.

And on the desk, the book waited.

For the next reader.

# XX

# Shadows Through The Lens

The world felt wrong.

Ana sat at the edge of her bed, Layla's old scarf clutched in her hands. The lavender scent—faint and fading—still lingered in the threads, but it was getting harder to remember the way her voice sounded, the exact curve of her smile, the small way she tilted her head when she was thinking hard.

Outside, the town of Maplewood looked unchanged. The sun spilled over the sidewalks, kids biked past, and Mrs. Collins was out watering her roses. But to Ana, everything felt hollow.

Because Layla was gone.

Not just gone—erased.

Ana had rushed to Layla's house that morning, heart pounding with dread and disbelief. She rang the doorbell three times before Ayaan answered, munching on cereal, looking groggy and disoriented.

"Ana?" he blinked. "Hey. What's up?"

"Is Layla home?" she asked, chest tight.

He frowned. "Who?"

Her heart cracked. "Layla. Your sister."

Ayaan stared at her, confused. "I don't have a sister."

Ana's knees buckled slightly. "Ayaan, don't joke. Please."

He shrugged. "I swear I don't know what you're talking about. Are you okay?"

Their mother came to the door next, smiling kindly. "Ana! How are you, sweetheart? Is everything alright?"

"I... I just needed to see Layla."

Mrs. Singh tilted her head. "Layla?"

Ana stared into her eyes and saw nothing. Not even the faintest glimmer of recognition. "I'm sorry," she murmured, stepping back. "I must've... I think I have the wrong house."

She stumbled away, breath ragged, tears sliding down her cheeks before she could stop them.

They didn't remember. Her own family.

It was happening—just like Mr. Williams warned.

By the time she reached the edge of the woods, Ana found Ryan sitting on the broken bench by the creek. He looked like he hadn't slept. His hands were red, raw from gripping the stone wall at the cemetery.

"She's not in the yearbooks anymore," he said hollowly. "I checked the digital archive. Every picture—she's gone. I even went to Principal Harris."

Ana sank down beside him.

"She asked me if I was feeling alright," he muttered. "Said there was never a Layla Singh enrolled at Riverstone High."

Ana wiped her tears, but they kept coming. "Her parents don't remember her. Even Ayaan. Her own mother smiled at me like I was a stranger."

Ryan turned to her, his eyes rimmed red. "Are we going crazy?"

Ana shook her head slowly. "No. We remember. That has to mean something."

They sat there for what felt like hours. The wind rustled the trees gently. Somewhere in the distance, a dog barked. The world moved on, unaware that it had lost someone irreplaceable.

Ana finally spoke. "We have to fight this."

Ryan turned to her.

"She was here, Ryan. I have photos. I still have some, even if some arc fading. I don't know why I can still see them, but I can."

She pulled out her camera and flicked through the screen. Group shots, hallway moments, park days. Layla laughing, Layla serious, Layla watching them with that quietly amused expression she always had.

"She mattered," Ana whispered. "And if the world won't remember her, then we will."

Ryan stared at the screen, a shaky breath escaping him. "What do we do?"

Ana looked up. Her grief had not gone—but underneath it now burned something fierce. A resolve.

"We document everything. We make it impossible to forget her."

---

The attic above Ryan's garage had become their base of grief.

It was quiet, filled with the soft scent of cedarwood and forgotten childhood games. Ryan sat cross-legged on the floor, Layla's journal in front of him—one Ana had found tucked inside her backpack, the last belonging no one else seemed to notice or remember.

He hadn't opened it yet.

He couldn't.

Instead, he stared at the edges of the leather-bound book, his mind aching with thoughts of her. Every detail of Layla's face danced behind his eyes—how her eyebrows knitted when she was annoyed, the way she tugged at her sleeves when nervous, the light in her eyes when she talked about stories that made the world feel like magic.

That light was gone now. And the world felt darker without it.

Ana sat across from him, sifting through her printed photographs. She had spent hours printing every image where Layla appeared, watching helplessly as some slowly faded no matter what she did.

"This one still has her," Ana murmured, holding up a picture of the three of them at the fall carnival. Layla had been laughing, her hair caught in the wind, cotton candy in her hand.

Ryan took it gently. His fingers trembled. "I remember that night."

"She was scared of the Ferris wheel," Ana smiled faintly. "But she still went on. For you."

Ryan's voice cracked. "She held my hand so tightly. Said it was the most terrifying five minutes of her life, and that she'd do it again if it meant seeing the view."

He closed his eyes, the memory stabbing deep.

"You ever think," he whispered, "that maybe if we hadn't gotten close... if I hadn't kissed her... maybe the book wouldn't have taken her?"

Ana didn't answer right away. Then, she said softly, "If love is what brought her closer to the curse, then it only proves how strong she was. Because she didn't run."

"But I should've done more," Ryan said, the pain blooming in his chest. "I should've fought it with her harder. I should've believed sooner. I should've been with her that night."

His breath shuddered as he leaned forward, head in his hands.

"I still hear her voice," he whispered. "I wake up expecting a text. I... I still wait for her in the hallway at school, and then I remember—she's gone. And no one even feels it."

Ana moved beside him and wrapped her arms around him. He broke down, the tears falling heavy and uncontrolled.

"She's not a ghost to us," Ana said through her own tears. "And we are not going to let her fade. Not completely."

They stayed like that for a long time—two broken hearts anchoring each other in the storm of forgetting.

---

They began their quiet rebellion at twilight.

Ana and Ryan snuck through Maplewood like ghosts, tracing the places Layla once loved—trying to stitch her back into the fabric of the town, as if presence alone could undo forgetting.

First was The Lantern.

The library had always smelled of old pages and sun-warmed wood. They slipped in through the side door Ana had learned to unlock after hours—Mr. Williams' key still dangling on the ribbon Layla once wore in her hair.

The silence inside was different now. Hollow. As if it, too, missed someone.

Ryan stood by the counter where Layla first found the cursed book. "She told me this place felt like it had secrets breathing through the walls," he said, voice soft.

Ana raised her camera. "Let's find them."

Click.

Next was the park bench—the one by the creek where Layla would sit and read. Where she kissed Ryan for the first time, just before the rain started.

He sat there now, shoulders hunched, eyes distant. Ana captured him like that. Not for the memory. For the grief.

"Why are we doing this?" he asked. "She's gone, Ana."

"No," she said, firm. "She's not forgotten. Not by us. And I believe that matters."

Click.

Last, they returned to Riverstone High, breaking in through the back stairwell door before dawn. The halls were cold and echoing, lockers standing like empty sentinels. Layla's locker, 212, had no nameplate now.

But Ana opened it anyway. And inside, tucked in the upper corner, was something neither of them expected—a dried lavender flower, pressed into the crevice. A memory fossilized.

Ryan ran a shaking hand across the metal. "She was real."

Click.

Their final stop was The Lantern, just as the sun began to rise.

Ana guided Ryan to the aisle where the book first called Layla. Her fingers hesitated on the camera's shutter.

"Maybe she's still here. If there's even a trace of her left... the lens will know."

She took the photo.

Just one.

No filters. No edits.

When they got back to Ana's, she uploaded it immediately. The image loaded slowly—grainy in the early morning light.

Layla was there.

Faint, tear-streaked, and turned slightly away—facing the shelf, her hand grazing the spine of a book. A ripple in the ordinary.

Ryan sank to his knees.

"She was trying to tell us goodbye," he choked.

Ana printed it.

Framed it in soft wood.

And together, they returned it to the shelf where it all began.

They left the photo there, alone and waiting.

By the next morning, it had faded. Slowly, like mist caught by the sun.

But Ana remembered. Ryan remembered.

And that was enough—for now.

---

Ana sat cross-legged in her room, surrounded by photographs. Some had already begun to fade, others remained intact—small miracles captured in shutter clicks. She held one of Layla on her birthday, frosting on her nose, eyes squinting in laughter.

She set up her phone and hit record.

Her voice, when it came, was soft. Honest.

"Hey, Layla. It's Ana."

She paused, swallowing the lump in her throat.

"I don't know if you can hear this. I don't even know if you... still exist like this anymore. But I wanted to talk to you anyway. Because I remember."

She picked up the photo gently.

"They don't know what they lost. Your mom baked brownies last night and didn't remember you loved the corner pieces. Ayaan's room doesn't even have your drawings anymore. Your locker is just metal now."

Her voice cracked.

"But you're not just gone. You're… stitched into everything, like invisible thread. I see you in the shadows at the library. In the scent of lavender on my jacket. In the way Ryan looks like he's always missing something."

She glanced toward her window. The sun was rising again.

"I don't know how long I'll keep remembering. Maybe that's how this thing works—it eats away at memory until even I forget. But I'm fighting it. And I think… I think you would've done the same for me."

She hit stop.

The voice note saved quietly, tucked into a folder on her phone labeled For Layla.

---

Ryan stood by the creek again.

This time he held the origami paper boat Layla had once shown him how to fold. On it, he'd written the words: You were my beginning.

He knelt by the water's edge.

"She said I made her feel real," he murmured. "But she's the one who made me believe in something bigger than just routine and noise."

The water lapped at his shoes.

Ryan released the boat. Watched it float—delicately, stubbornly.

"Goodbye, Layla."

The paper drifted away.

And with it, something inside him settled—not peace, not acceptance. But love, in its most stubborn, enduring form.

---

That night, Ana returned to The Lantern one last time.

The framed photo was gone.

In its place sat an old book.

The title was blank.

But when she opened the cover, there on the first page, was a single name.

Layla Singh.

And beneath it: She was real.

Ana closed it with trembling hands. Her tears returned—this time, not from grief, but from something gentler.

Remembrance.

The shelf seemed quieter afterward. Almost... content.

# XXI
## The First Page

The story shifts.

Morning arrives in Maplewood with a gentle stillness. The storm has passed, but something deeper has quieted. The streets are clean, the air crisp, and the town carries on—unchanged, unaware of the memories it has let go.

The camera drifts.

Past Riverstone High, where Layla once walked the halls.

Past the park bench where Ana and Ryan sat, clinging to a memory the world no longer shared.

Past the Singh household, where Ayaan eats breakfast and Mrs. Singh hums a tune neither of them knows once belonged to Layla.

And then, it finds The Lantern.

The library stands timeless, as if untouched by all the tragedies and truths it has held inside. Its windows shimmer in the morning sun, and dust particles swirl in the slanting beams of light. The quiet feels sacred here—like a place between chapters, where a breath is held before something begins again.

Inside, Mr. Williams walks the aisles with slow, practiced steps. His fingers brush over the spines of books that have seen generations pass through. He pauses at one shelf—the same shelf.

The one where it began.

He rests his hand on it.

The space between two books feels denser than air, as though memory has weight, even when forgotten.

A soft bell chimes.

The front door creaks open.

Mr. Williams turns toward the sound.

A new girl steps inside. Her hair is in a short braid, her expression uncertain but curious. She wears a forest-green jacket with sleeves pushed to her elbows and a canvas bag slung over her shoulder. She hesitates in the doorway, taking in the scent of old paper, wood polish, and something just barely metallic in the air.

She doesn't know why she's here. Only that she was meant to be.

Drawn.

Her feet move without direction, taking her past the checkout desk, past poetry and plays, until she reaches a corner where the light seems softer and the silence deeper.

Her eyes settle on it.

A single book. Worn leather. Cracked spine. No title.

She reaches out.

Fingers brush the cover—and the air shifts, almost like a sigh.

Behind her, Mr. Williams watches, silent and still.

She opens the book.

The pages whisper as they turn.

And then—

The first line appears on the page, ink forming slowly, deliberately:

*""Once upon a time, there was a girl named...""*

She stares.
Somewhere, the light flickers.
And the story begins again.
Fade to black.

### THE END...

# Epilogue

There are stories that end with a lesson.

Some end with a kiss, a promise, or the echo of a final heartbeat.

But some stories—the oldest ones, the quietest ones—do not end at all.

They loop.

Whisper.

Rewrite.

Somewhere in Maplewood, a girl once lived. Or maybe she didn't. Maybe her story was borrowed, built from ink and memory and silence. Maybe she walked the halls of Riverstone High, laughed with her best friend at Starbucks, fell in love beneath fading skies.

Or maybe she only existed on a page.

But for Ana, her laughter still flickers at the edge of dreams.

For Ryan, the feeling of her hand in his lingers in empty hallways.

And for those who know where to look—those who dare to remember—there are signs.

A photo that refuses to stay blank.

A bench that feels warm even in winter.

A page that turns itself in a book no one remembers borrowing.

Because the book remembers.

It always remembers.

And when the next name is written...

It begins again.